# The 1 of US

# LORI FOSTER

## MAISEY YATES

**KENSINGTON**
PUBLISHING CORP.

kensingtonbooks.com

KENSINGTON BOOKS are published by

Kensington Publishing Corp.
900 Third Avenue
New York, NY 10022

All Kensington titles, imprints, and distributed lines are available at special quantity discounts for bulk purchases for sales promotion, premiums, fund-raising, educational, or institutional use.

This book is a work of fiction. Names, characters, businesses, organizations, places, events, and incidents either are the product of the author's imagination or are used fictitiously. Any resemblance to actual persons, living or dead, events, or locales is entirely coincidental.

To the extent that the image or images on the cover of this book depict a person or persons, such person or persons are merely models, and are not intended to portray any character or characters featured in the book.

Special book excerpts or customized printings can also be created to fit specific needs. For details, write or phone the office of the Kensington Sales Manager: Kensington Publishing Corp., 900 Third Avenue, New York, NY 10022. Attn. Sales Department. Phone: 1-800-221-2647.

Kensington and the K logo Reg. U.S. Pat. & TM Off.

ISBN: 978-1-4967-5416-5 (ebook)
ISBN: 978-1-4967-5415-8

First Kensington Trade Paperback Printing: April 2025

10 9 8 7 6 5 4 3 2 1

Printed in the United States of America

# Contents

The Odd Couple

*Lori Foster*

1


Force of Nature

*Maisey Yates*

119

# The Odd Couple

## Lori Foster

# Chapter 1

"Excuse me?"

Ford Caruso was enjoying a much-needed break with his friends after building a deck to encircle his pool, so it took a second to realize someone had intruded. He glanced up and saw his amazingly hot neighbor, Skye Fairchild.

She normally didn't come over to chat. He'd wave, she'd wave. Occasionally, they'd share a short conversation from their yards. Once, after a storm, one of her tree limbs had landed mostly in his yard. She'd been out there in the still-drizzling rain, trying unsuccessfully to drag it into her yard, when he'd walked out and taken over—despite her protests.

Silly woman. He'd had it cut up in no time, and together they'd gotten the pieces stacked on her wood pile. They'd talked a lot then, all of it superficial and easy, but she hadn't lingered once the work was done.

On another occasion when he'd left the house in a hurry and his garage door hadn't closed, she'd done it for him. When he'd come home, she'd walked over to let him know, in case anyone had seen her go into his garage to hit the door button and quickly dash out beneath the closing door. Again, they'd chatted. Again, it had been friendly and easy, but when he'd invited her in, she'd merely thanked him and gone home.

Right next door to him.

It felt spectacularly humbling to have such a gorgeous neighbor . . . who, from all indications, wasn't in the least interested in him.

She was always precisely polite, without a single lingering glance or hint of interest. They'd gotten to know each other over the last twelve months, but only in a superficial way. She remained in the friendly acquaintance department. A helpful neighbor. Upbeat and independent.

Through her actions—and lack of actions—she'd made it clear that she didn't want to be a *close* neighbor. No flirting. No teasing.

Fine by him.

He didn't need to win her over.

Yet here she stood, the setting sun creating a halo around her incredible body and long, wavy, fawn-colored hair. She wore a black top that perfectly hugged her breasts, khaki shorts that showed off lightly tanned legs, and a friendly smile on her face.

He, Marcus, Knox, and Bray all stared at her.

Her smile never faltered. "I'm sorry to interrupt. I didn't mean to put an end to your"—one small hand gestured, encompassing the four of them, the pool behind them, and their drinks—"party? Or just a gathering?"

"A visit," Ford said. "Just a visit." If she thought it was a party, she might want to join them. "What's up?"

"Are any of you single?"

Silently, Bray and Marcus, who'd each recently married, pointed at Ford. Even Knox, the ass, pointed, and Knox was single, too.

Feeling his neck go hot, Ford stood. Rather than be put on the spot, he switched gears. "Why are you asking?"

"Well, you see, I need a little helping hand. For . . . oh, an hour maybe? Probably not any longer than that. Only it wouldn't be right to ask a married man to help, so I figured I'd get that sorted out upfront."

Smiling, Knox came to his feet. "Gotta say, I'm intrigued."

Marcus, also wearing a smile, joined him. "Same."

Bray, who was a bit of a hard-ass, was the last to come forward. Always astute, he guessed, "You need help with an unwanted visitor?"

Relieved, she gave Bray a blinding smile. "Exactly. He'll be here soon, and I've been stewing and stewing, trying to figure out the best way to handle things. Seeing you guys out here, I decided, why not ask? I mean, the four of you are just hanging out, right?" And then, with a charming grin, she added, "It would be a really huge help."

As an MMA fighter, Bray Barlow was by far the brawniest of the four men. "What kind of help are we talking about?"

Scrunching up a nose that was slightly thick at the bridge, yet still suited her otherwise perfect face, she said, "Nothing violent, I promise. See, I have an ex. . . . Well, he's an ex-creep but he used to be a sort-of-boyfriend."

With a grin, Knox Nial asked, "How is one a sort-of-boyfriend?"

"Convenient?" She said it like a question. "Easy to look at, but not great to talk to. Handy when I needed a date for a function." She waved that off. "Anyway, we had an agreement, but that arrangement isn't working out anymore. It started to get very inconvenient, if you know what I mean."

"No," Ford said, irked on behalf of all men. "I don't."

"Let's just say he forgot the agreement."

"He was aware of it?" Knox asked, his brows raised.

Chin tucking, she drew back. "Of course. I was upfront about everything."

With sympathy, probably for the guy, Bray said, "But he got invested?"

She shrugged. "He wanted to get serious, I didn't, so I ended things a couple of weeks ago. He's been a little"—she scrunched her nose again and searched for a word—"persistent."

"How persistent?" Marcus asked.

"Wherever I go, he happens to be there." She waved the behavior off as trivial. "We frequent some of the same places, so that wouldn't be a problem except that he acts as if we're still together, and I've made it clear we're not."

Meaning the mistreated ex was getting in the way of her making a new hookup? Too bad for her.

Yeah, Ford tried to convince himself of that. Wasn't working.

From what he knew of Skye so far, she was independent. Nice. Considerate. She wouldn't abuse the guy, then mosey on like it didn't matter.

And even if she did, the guy ought to accept her decision and move on.

Continuing, Skye said, "The unfortunate part of all this is that he has a few things at my house, and he just texted that he's stopping by. I tried texting back to say I'd bring his stuff to him, but of course there's no reply. I tried calling, too, but no answer."

"I've never seen a guy at your house."

Everyone looked at Ford.

Yeah, maybe he shouldn't have said that. Wasn't like he kept watch on her or anything.

His buddies eyed him as if they'd never seen him before. Skye just lifted a shoulder. "You leave early for work, right? And a lot of times you only get home to turn around and head back out again."

So . . . did that mean she was keeping watch on him? Ford wasn't at all sure how he felt about that.

As if she expected the ex to show up at any second, Skye glanced back toward the street. "Once he's here, it's going to be hard for me to get rid of him."

Marcus Bareden, a cop, made the obvious suggestion. "Maybe what you need to do is call the police."

"Oh, no." Dark blue eyes widening, she gave them her attention again. "I wouldn't want to bother the police just because he's being a pest. He's not dangerous or anything." She came closer, bringing with her the scent of sunshine and spice and all things delicious. "I have a different idea, but it requires a single guy."

Again, everyone looked at Ford. He scowled back at them. Still calmly reasonable, Bray asked, "A single guy to . . . ?"

"Pretend he's my new guy. See, any one of you would do. I mean, Clyde would probably be intimidated by all the good looks and buff bods. Totally extra, if you know what I mean."

Like a bunch of preening buffoons, his friends grinned.

"He's persistent because I haven't started dating anyone else. I'm thinking he'd take one look at any of you and accept that he has no chance of getting me back, and then he'd finally, *hopefully*, move on." She put her hands together in mock prayer. "I promise it'll be painless. All you'd need to do is hang around while he's there, smile as if you like me—"

"We do like you," Knox said, which prompted immediate agreement from the others.

"Aw, thanks, guys." She beamed at them. "Wow, I should have intro'd myself before jumping in for favors, right? Sorry."

Actually, Ford should have done that, but she'd taken him by surprise, showing up as she had, and then asking who was single.

Coming closer still, her slim hand extended, she said, "I'm Skye Fairchild. I live next door."

Marcus took her hand first. "Marcus Bareden, happily married, but still glad to help if I can. In fact, my wife would be the first to insist."

"He's a cop," Bray said, taking her hand next. "I'm Bray

Barlow, fortunately married though it wasn't easy." They all laughed because, seriously, Bray had fought hard to win over Karen, and now they were both delirious about being together. "Also glad to lend a hand."

"He's an MMA fighter," Knox explained. "Plenty of muscle if you like that sort of thing."

"Which my wife does," Bray said with satisfaction.

"Wow, a fighter, a cop." Skye looked at them with awe. "You guys are impressive."

"I'm Knox Nial, just a roofer, but ditto on what the others said." He slung his arm around Ford. "I take it you know Ford Caruso, the one who lives here?"

She gave him a wary glance. "We've met."

"He's a pharmaceutical rep," Knox explained—very unnecessarily. "A little too slick, too quick to schmooze, but still an okay guy."

"There's no *just* to it." Ford nudged Knox, hoping to deflect attention away from himself. "Knox has worked in his dad's company since he was a kid. Don't let him fool you. He's strong as an ox."

Skye's attention went back and forth between Knox and Ford. "So I was right? You two are a couple?"

Ford sputtered. "You've lived next door to me for a year now!"

"Has it been a year?"

She knew damn well it had. "You've seen me bring women here."

Her nose lifted. "I don't make note of your comings and goings."

He took great pleasure in pointing out the obvious. "You just said you noticed me coming and going."

"To work and such. I don't pay attention to your dates."

What bull. They each had nice yards, but there wasn't that

much space between their houses. "There's no way you've missed every woman."

She lifted a shoulder. "I've seen you with a few. So? You didn't seem as close to any of them as you are with him." She nodded at Knox.

With a totally different attitude, Knox slung his heavy arm around Ford's shoulders again. "You don't think I could do better than him?"

Ford ignored his grin. "You wish."

"I know all his worst habits, and believe me, he has plenty. I would never live with him. As a friend, though, he's not a bad guy."

"Gee, thanks for the glowing endorsement." Ford shoved him away. "I'm not into guys. How about you?"

"Sure," Skye said. "But not my ex, and not you guys, either."

Clutching his heart, Knox lamented, "Damned by association."

"I'm glad you're finding this all so amusing." To Ford, it was just confusing. "He's a friend—though that could end at any moment."

"You two bicker like a married couple."

Loving it, Knox hauled Ford nearer again, practically crushing him into his side. "How women put up with him, I have no idea."

Again, Ford freed himself. His brain was working overtime trying to figure out Skye's motivation. In all the time she'd lived next door, never, not once, had she just moseyed over for a favor, much less a "single guy" favor. To him, it felt suspicious.

Apparently, Knox had a different take, because he rubbed his hands together in anticipation. "So who's it to be? One of us going to help her out?"

"As a cop," Marcus said, "I should only get involved in an official capacity, but she doesn't want that."

"Sorry, no," she said. "The police have enough to do without concerning themselves with my social calamities."

"If he needs to be pulverized"—Bray shrugged—"I'd be happy to help."

"I promise he doesn't." Skye grinned. "But if it's ever an issue, I know who to call."

Knox opened his mouth—and his phone dinged. He pulled it from his pocket, glanced at the screen, and said, "Sorry, but I gotta roll."

Frowning, Ford asked, "Everything okay?"

"Yeah. An elderly homeowner just asked if I could come by tonight instead of tomorrow to give an estimate on a new roof. Her husband's medical appointment changed." He texted a reply, then glanced up at the sun, which was hanging low in the sky. "I'd better get to it."

Knowing Knox would always put his customers first, Ford watched him head back to his lawn chair to grab up his shirt and shrug into it.

"Well." Skye looked at him. "I guess that leaves only you, but if you'd rather not, I promise I understand."

"I'd rather not."

Her smile only slipped a tiny bit.

Marcus and Bray glared at him as if he'd just kicked a puppy.

From behind him, Knox growled, "Screw it. I'll tell the homeowner I can't make it after all."

With a roll of his eyes, Ford gave up. "I'd rather not—*but I will*." There. He'd be benevolent. He'd play her savior. He'd lend a hand to scare off her nuisance ex. Feeling selflessly smug, he bestowed a smile on her.

But this time, Skye was the one to balk. "I'm not sure Clyde would believe that you like me. You're a pharmaceutical rep, not an actor." Heaving a sigh, she said, "I thank you all, but I knew it was a long shot anyway. I promise, it'll be fine." She started backing up. "No worries at all. I've totally got this." Going for a look of confidence, she said, "It was great meeting you all. Again, so sorry I interrupted."

Then she had the audacity to turn around and sashay off. And yes, the woman absolutely did sashay, whether it was intentional or not.

Ford watched as she crossed the yard and reentered her house through the back door. When he realized everyone was staring after her, he said, "Ahem, married men, remember?"

"Go to hell," Marcus said, looking extremely disappointed in him. "I wasn't ogling her. I'm worried."

"I ogled," Knox admitted. "Not sure I've ever seen a supermodel up close and personal."

"She's not," Ford groused. He seemed to remember mention of her being a buyer or merchandiser or something like that.

"She's model-worthy, and nice, too. Which makes me wonder what's wrong with you."

Ford ignored him.

Bray said, "I was watching her, waiting for you to stop her. Now I just realize how bullheaded you are for letting her walk away."

If Bray wasn't such an enormous ape, Ford might take offense. "Me, bullheaded? Am I the only one who sees that for the trap it was?"

Marcus and Bray shared a look.

"They're doing it," Knox said. "That silent exchange thing that means they're seeing something we don't see."

Well, hell. Marcus and Bray had both come from abusive homes, so they often picked up on clues that others might miss.

Ford, however, wasn't as intuitive as they.

Was Skye afraid of her ex? She hadn't seemed to be. Surely a woman as gorgeous as she could have her pick of heroes to hang around and play protector.

Provided she wanted that sort of thing. She'd claimed the ex was only a nuisance. That she didn't want to get serious. But maybe he'd read the situation all wrong. If she'd truly only wanted a friendly neighbor to lend a hand, then yeah, that made him a jerk. Damn it, now he was starting to feel guilty.

"He's coming around," Knox said low, as if confiding a secret to the others. "I know the way his mind works."

Bray said, "You know, you two do your own silent communicating. Skye was right about that. You could pass yourselves off as a couple."

"Hate to repeat myself, but he's not my type." With mock regret, Knox said, "Too fussy." With a whack to Ford's shoulder, he added, "Do the right thing, and let me know later how it goes."

"Yeah, all right."

Grinning, Marcus said, "I gotta go, too, but *call me.*"

Ford reached for him, but Bray got in his way. "Ease up there, Gas Pedal. You're pissed at yourself, not anyone else."

True. After glancing at Skye's house, Ford blew out a breath. "I wouldn't have hurt him—much."

Marcus snorted. None of them took such threats seriously—they'd been friends for too long. Sharing insults was practically the same as a friendly greeting.

Bray said, "Jokes aside, keep us informed. If her ex turns out to be a bigger problem than she thinks, don't take any chances."

Since Bray's wife had dealt with the ex from hell, Ford understood Bray's concern. "It'll be fine, but thanks." It was another couple of minutes before his three friends departed. With his thoughts churning, he gave himself a few minutes to mentally prepare, going around back and tidying up, as always taking pleasure in what was his.

He'd worked hard to earn a good-paying job, a nice car, and a house. For as long as he could remember, he'd wanted those things. He'd wanted autonomy. He'd needed to prove—to himself more than anyone else—that he was different. Reliable. Productive. Honorable. Upstanding.

At twenty-seven, he'd reached the majority of his goals.

Giving himself a pat on the back, he took in his rectangular, aboveground pool. Not super fancy, but it looked great now that they'd built a deck all the way around it. There was room to add a small patio table and chairs, a few lounge chairs, maybe even a potted plant. He envisioned many happy hours lounging in the cool water this summer.

He'd just put away the folding chairs when he heard a car pull in and everything inside him went on alert.

Jogging to the side of the yard, he saw a slick red Mustang in Skye's driveway.

In a split second, Ford made up his mind. He sprinted around to her back door and started to knock, but then he saw her sitting at her kitchen table, her head in her hands, her long hair streaming forward, and her shoulders a little slumped.

It was the oddest thing, but something that felt remarkably like guilt gave his heart a firm kick. His conscience, too. The dual assault was damned uncomfortable, and he didn't like it. He didn't want anything about her to make him uncomfortable.

Worse, other body parts did strange things that made absolutely no sense in this situation. Lungs expanding, muscles twitching . . . Awareness sparked.

Well, hell.

Knowing he only had a moment, he rapped his knuckles on the frame of the sliding door and said through the screen, "Mind if I come in?"

She jerked around so fast she nearly fell off her seat. That long, sun-kissed, honey-colored hair swung out around her.

Her eyes rounded, then narrowed. "I let you off the hook." She even managed a smile. "If your friends pressured you, they shouldn't have. Everything is fine, so—"

"The ex is here, and I want to help. Trust me, I'll have no problem playing my role." The natural attraction he felt for this beautiful woman, regardless of whether she was in trouble or not, would aid him.

Straightening her shoulders, she said, "Not sure I believe you."

He couldn't blame her. Cautiously, in case she protested, he slid the screen open. "You should keep that locked."

One dark brow lifted.

"Okay?" He stopped a few feet from her. "If you want me to leave, say so now. Otherwise, let's do this."

Lips that were, maybe, just a *little* too full, slowly curled. "You're not a martyr. You don't need to do this."

Yeah, he most definitely did. Later, he'd figure out this new altruistic bent. For now, he wanted to get on with it. "This is me, entirely willing."

She scoffed. "Clyde will see right through you, and that'll just make it worse."

"I promise he won't." Crouching down in front of her, he smiled. "Want me to convince you first?" His smile was slow and intimate as his gaze moved over her face. "I can, you know."

Her lips parted and her eyes softened.

In a gruff whisper, he asked, "Am I convincing?"

Skye disliked the way she suddenly felt, a little twitchy, a little too warm, and definitely aware in a sensual way, but whatever. Though he'd made his objections clear, Ford was here now, likely prodded by his more chivalrous friends, but so what? He'd do as well as anyone, and their association would be so temporary as to practically not exist.

Reminding herself that it was all for show, she let out a shaky breath. "If this goes off the rails—"

"It won't," he promised, and stood again.

When the knock sounded on her front door, he caught her fingers in his much larger, slightly rough, and incredibly warm hand.

Oh, not good. His touch was electrifying, though she tried to hide her reaction. Instead of feeling impersonal, the connection was far too intimate—at least for her. Ford didn't seem all that affected.

The second she gained her feet, he led her through the kitchen, past her small dining room, into the living room, and to the entry door. Of course, he knew the way. Their houses had similar layouts, but with different exteriors. Hers was siding, his brick. Her landscaping was new and still small, his was lush and well-manicured. And now he had that amazing deck that made his pool a beautiful feature in his backyard. Her yard was more shaded, with several big trees.

"What's his name again?" Ford asked quietly.

"Clyde. Why?"

Another knock sounded, followed by the doorbell.

He released her, saying, "Go ahead and let him in."

Incredulous, she said low, "That's what I'm doing." She unlocked not one, but two locks. Ford said nothing else, but as she pulled the door open, he draped a long arm around her shoulders, smiled brightly, and literally took over.

Before she could get out a single word, he said, "Hey, Clyde, right?" He stepped aside to let Clyde in, and as he had her pinned to his side, she moved with him. "Nice ride you have. Is it new?"

Bewildered, Clyde stared at him. "Who the hell are you?"

"Neighbor," Ford said, his smile still in place. "Friend. Confidant. Escort." Lifting his brows, he added, "Admirer. Currently *the one*. You know what I mean."

Bristling, Clyde said, "No, I don't."

"Ah, man. Sucks for you."

Skye nearly choked. Good grief. Where had her standoffish neighbor gone? He was now the man she'd often heard joking with his friends.

She kind of liked both personas.

Ford hugged her into his side with an overdose of affection. "Skye told me you had to pick up a few things?"

"I have it all right here." Darting away from Ford, she went to the couch and lifted a box. "Two CDs, your charging cord, a hat, the book you wanted me to read, sunglasses, ear buds, and your pen." She met Clyde's gaze and stated, "Everything you left in my car." For some reason, she wanted Ford to know that Clyde hadn't been in her house.

After considering everything she'd said to him and his friends, she'd realized how bad it had made her sound. Like a total user. Like someone who'd taken advantage of Clyde and then ruthlessly dumped him.

Not the way it had happened, and though she'd assumed that one visit with them was all she'd ever have, she'd hated to leave them with that impression.

Then Ford had showed up after all, and now here she was, with both men staring at her over the way she'd listed the inventory.

Ready to end the farce, she thrust the box at Clyde.

He took it only to set it aside. "I want to talk, Skye."

God, this was so awkward. Gently, because she did feel bad, Skye said, "We've done enough talking, I think."

When Clyde started to step forward, Ford got in his way. "Sorry, man." His tone was still cordial. "She says no."

Clyde was not a small man. He was muscular, maybe as much so as Bray. He intimidated a lot of people.

Apparently, not Ford.

They were nearly the same height, but the similarities ended there. Clyde was big and bulky, Ford was lean and athletic.

Clyde's dark hair and eyes were a stark contrast to Ford's blond hair and mesmerizing green eyes.

Mesmerizing? No, that was ridiculous. Nothing mesmerizing about the man at all.

Interrupting their silent stare down, she came forward—and was immediately snagged again by Ford, who treated her to a warm kiss on her temple.

"What she says, goes," Ford explained. "And we both know she's been clear."

Clyde's expression hardened. "I'm not buying it."

"It?" Ford asked.

"The idea of you two together. The touching and kissing."

Her heart seized up. Of course, he knew better. In a moment of weakness, she'd explained a few things to Clyde. Now he'd use that knowledge against her? No, no, no. Hoping to reason with him, she said, "Clyde—"

"Maybe if you weren't laying it on so thick, I'd be convinced. I mean, new sidekick? Yeah, that I'd believe. Skye doesn't like to attend parties alone. But this?" He gestured at Ford's arm around her. "I was with her first, so I know better."

Wishing the floor would swallow her up, Skye tried to withdraw.

Instead of letting her go, Ford tightened his hold. "Whatever you think you know," he said, his voice low, "I suggest you get your belongings and get out."

Dismissing him as unimportant, Clyde stared only at Skye. "I don't know what game you're playing, but have you laid out the rules to him?"

No, she hadn't, because as he'd said, this show with Ford wasn't real. And she'd been right. Clyde wasn't fooled.

In an oddly protective gesture, Ford stepped in front of her, which meant Clyde had to step back. "Rules that applied to *you*," Ford said. "Seriously, dude, I'm sorry. You got stuck in the friend zone, and that had to burn, but it's over. Just gather up your pride and go."

Furious, Clyde shook his head. "Not that easy." To Skye, he said, "I'll see you at the restaurant next week, and at Mel's party after that." He completely ignored Ford. "And whenever I shop."

In other words, he intended to haunt her everywhere she went. Would she ever be rid of him?

Bunching his muscles, Ford warned, "Those plans sound an awful lot like stalking."

"Stalking?" he scoffed. "Her friends are my friends, and vice versa. We're both invited to the party. And I've bought plenty of gifts at the boutique." His smile was far from friendly. "Isn't that right, Skye?"

Things were getting completely out of control. Having another man around hadn't discouraged Clyde at all. He actually seemed to feel challenged to prove something.

She was pondering how to end this visit when Ford did the unthinkable.

He stepped into Clyde's space.

Though his tone was casual, antagonism charged the air. "One way or another, your ass is going on the other side of the door. You decide how that's going to happen."

"*Ford.*" Hadn't she made it clear that this wasn't to be a violent confrontation? Clyde wasn't a pushover; anyone could see that. Ford, however, spoke as if he didn't have a single doubt of his own ability.

What in the world had gotten into him?

Unimpressed, Clyde laughed, but he also took a step back. "Don't worry, Skye. I won't mess up his face." He grabbed up the box, then paused to stare at her. "He doesn't know you like I do. He doesn't understand your insecurities. If he did, he wouldn't be here."

Probably true. She couldn't look at Ford, but then, he wasn't looking at her either. All his attention was fixed on Clyde.

"When he walks," Clyde added, "and we both know he will, I'll still be around. Give me a call."

"Why don't you hold your breath?" Done being passive in this awful confrontation, Skye pressed forward to stand beside Ford. "I'd always thought you were nice, but you taught me better, didn't you?"

For only a second, Clyde appeared hurt. Then he went out the door, and she closed it firmly behind him, turned the lock, and stepped away. A few seconds later, they heard him gun the engine, back out of her driveway, and accelerate away.

Ford didn't move. Shoulders knotted, his hands in fists, he continued to face the door. "You would have faced that asshole alone."

She had no idea what to say to him. She couldn't think with her heart punching so hard inside her chest. "I could have handled it."

"And you would have, if I'd kept on being a dipshit."

Should she explain about Clyde? Could she explain?

No! She and Ford were friendly, but they weren't in any way close. Despite his being here now, she didn't owe him explanations.

Audibly inhaling and slowly exhaling, Ford pivoted to her with a good-natured smile as if all was fine and dandy in his world. "Well, good riddance. You were right about him. Definitely a nuisance. I'm glad my friends heckled me and that I came over."

Her thoughts scrambling this way and that, Skye struggled to make sense of his reaction. Had he really been furious, or just feigning that reaction for Clyde? No, looking into his eyes, she knew his anger hadn't been a sham. He was putting on a good show for her now.

She tried to think of how to respond, but all she could manage was a quiet, "Thank you. I appreciate the help."

"What are neighbors for, if not a little heavy lifting?"

Great attitude, but she couldn't let it go at that. "For the record, I didn't expect Clyde's reaction. Reluctance on his part, sure. But not"—she flapped her hand—"whatever that was."

"That was a guy who didn't want to take no for an answer."

Obviously, she hadn't known Clyde as well as she'd thought.

"I didn't mean to drag you into anything violent."

"Not sure you could. I mean, I'm twice your size. Remember the difficulty you had with that large limb? I'd be even tougher to drag."

Humor was nowhere in reach, so she only met his gaze and waited.

"Skye." Getting real, he said, "Not a big deal, okay? Bozos are everywhere, believe me. I've dealt with my fair share."

"You practically challenged him."

Still looking very calm, he said, "You have no idea how badly I wanted to. Bullies infuriate me. But hey, I'll survive the disappointment of letting him off easy."

See, *that.* Clearly, he assumed he'd have come out the victor, but how in the world could he think it would be that easy? "I've never seen Clyde so aggressive before. I swear, it wasn't what I expected."

"Some guys aren't great with rejection, and believe me, finding me here sharpened the sensation for him. He wanted you alone, he hoped to convince you, but he'll get over it."

This was all such a mess. She looked away, wishing she hadn't bothered him, wishing she hadn't opened the door to Clyde—wishing she'd never made the ridiculous arrangement with Clyde in the first place.

Touching her chin, Ford brought her gaze back to his. "Whatever you're dealing with in your life, it's your business. Clyde was an ass for trying to embarrass you." Releasing her, he held out his arms. "Look, this is me, unimpressed with him. You should be unimpressed, too."

Briefly, she closed her eyes, but she wasn't a coward. "Right. He can only bother me if I let him."

"True to a point. Emotionally, anyway. The thing is, I don't think he's going to back off completely. If you really want him to—"

"I do!" Surely, he didn't still doubt that. They'd just seen Clyde at his worst. "The shine wore off that friendship weeks ago, and that was before he acted like an obnoxious ape."

"Then could I make a suggestion?"

Guessing what he'd say, she went to her couch and sat down. "I can't involve the cops."

"Okay."

She chewed her bottom lip. "I should avoid the restaurant and skip the party." Even though she'd made those plans ages ago, and even though the party was part of her job, it was still—

"Wrong move," he said. "At least in my opinion." Taking a seat next to her, he got close, but didn't touch her. "You should never give in to bullies. They see it as encouragement and things get worse."

Recognizing the sincerity in his eyes, she nodded. "Okay. Then what?"

"You have to stand up to bullies."

"I tried that," she admitted, frowning at the memory. "It was awful. He caused a scene and embarrassed me."

"Were you alone or with a date?"

Maybe it was time she made a few things clear. "I was at a club with friends, no date though. That's how I prefer it."

"Okay, fair enough."

Wait, what? It couldn't be that easy. As soon as she saw his smile, she knew he had more to say.

"Another guy wasn't around because you're not interested. Understood. Can I just point out that going it alone isn't working great so far? That's why you visited me today, right?"

"I can't exactly deny it."

"So this is me, volunteering further. Feel free to use me."

Heated visuals flashed through her brain. "*Use* you?" Surely, he didn't mean that the way it sounded.

His voice went low and rough. "I wasn't offering up my body, so don't get ideas. It's this pretend stuff I can handle."

Trying to cover her reaction, she eyed him. "Your friends seemed to think even that would be difficult for you."

Jokingly putting his nose in the air, he stated, "Nothing with women is difficult for me."

That was so absurd, she laughed. How had she not known her neighbor was funny, too? "This whole situation is a mess, and still you're amusing."

"It's a gift."

Appreciating him more by the second, she said, "I agree."

His expression softened. "You have a dinner, and then a party, right?" When she nodded, he said, "So take me along. I can discourage your ape and ensure he can't bother you. He'll eventually get the message and tire of hanging around."

She wasn't at all convinced.

"The offer comes with no strings attached."

"Last time I tried that, I ended up with an obnoxious ape."

"Ah, so that explains Clyde. I did wonder."

"You thought I was awful, didn't you?"

Instead of denying it, he said, "Maybe a little. The good news is that I'm nothing like him. For whatever reason, you don't want to get involved. I probably have just as many reasons for feeling the same."

She listed two of those reasons easily enough. "You're a diehard bachelor, and you enjoy playing the field."

"Not precisely true, not all of it anyway."

"No?" she asked with a lot of skepticism.

"If you ever want to share stories, maybe we'll discuss it. Until then, let's just say we both have our reasons. In the meantime, we can hang out, right? I got a smile or two out of you, and even a laugh. My company won't be an awful hardship, and

Clyde doesn't intimidate me." He held out his hand. "What do you say?"

"Your offer is almost too good to be true."

He didn't retract his hand. "Then let me surprise you." Remembering the charge she'd felt last time she'd touched him, she should have been reluctant; instead, she felt only relief as she put her palm to his.

Keeping the handshake agreement brief, he said, "Give me all the details on your upcoming social calendar—that is, anything that involves Clyde. We'll make this work. I promise."

# Chapter 2

He had a week before he needed to visit her again, but that didn't stop Ford from noticing every damn time she stepped out to her yard, drove off in her car, or arrived back home. For the last five days, if he was around, he was aware of her.

Talking with her had become easier, though it was still pretty superficial. He kept thinking he needed to invite her to his pool, but that would cross a line, right?

Luckily his own schedule had been busy, so he hadn't been able to spend all his time focusing on her. Only about eighty percent or so. Much as he'd fought it, she even inhabited his dreams. Some of them were casual. Some . . . not so much.

Best dreams he'd had in a very long while.

Had to be from denying himself. With most women who caught his eye, he'd make the natural suggestion of getting together for mutual enjoyment. She'd either accept or he'd move on. Nothing with Skye was that simple.

Finally, with an evening free, he'd invited his friends over to enjoy the pool. June was hotter than usual this year and the water had already warmed comfortably. While everyone chatted around him, enjoying his new patio furniture and the usual camaraderie, Ford stewed.

He didn't like stewing, damn it. Again, he glanced over to Skye's house. Should he have invited her to join them? She knew the guys now and . . . No. She'd made it clear that she didn't want to get too friendly. Theirs was a business arrangement, period.

While he was attempting to convince himself of that, her back patio doors slid open, drawing his attention. Not even glancing their way, she stepped out in tan shorts and an army green halter, barefoot, and headed to the hose wrapped around a decorative hanger.

"He's staring," Knox said.

She was impossible to ignore now that he knew her a little better. Now that he'd touched her.

Now that he'd sensed her vulnerability and seen what she was up against with Clyde-the-obnoxious.

"Because she looks good." Bray, with Karen beside him, also watched as Skye watered the plants on her back patio.

"She's deliberately not looking at us." Marcus frowned at Ford and added, "Probably because he made her feel unwelcome."

Voice low and distracted, Ford said, "You already know I made it up to her."

Lucy, who was there with Marcus, left her chair, stepped down from the deck, and started across the yard.

Alarmed, Ford sat forward. "What is she doing?"

Karen smiled. "You already know the answer to that." She, too, left.

"Damn it," he hissed. "That's not our agreement." Skye didn't want his friends becoming her friends. She didn't even want him.

The two women stopped at the edge of his property. Lucy asked, "Skye, right?"

Looking up, Skye paused, then turned off her hose and walked over. Not even for a second did she glance at Ford. "Yes. Can I help you?"

Lucy gestured back at the men. "I'm Marcus's wife and a friend of Ford's. This is Karen, married to Bray."

Wincing, Skye said, "I hope I didn't overstep the other day. I asked right off about who was single and who wasn't."

With a laugh, Karen waved off her concern. "No problem at all. I'm glad you took the initiative. I had a similar situation once."

"Oh?"

"Then I trusted Bray, and that meant trusting all of them, because they definitely pull together."

Lucy said, "I was already one of the guys, so they were always around to lend me a hand."

Confusion left Skye floundering. "One of the guys?"

"A neighbor, a friend. We all regularly hung out together."

"Ah." Skye smiled softly. "I bet that was nice."

*What?* Ford felt himself frowning and didn't care. Hadn't she recently told him that she didn't want involvement? Okay, so she'd meant with him. Romantically. Whatever. His friends were a part of the deal.

"Now that I hang out with them, too, I can confirm that it's very nice," Karen said.

To Marcus and Bray, Ford grumbled, "Skye has to realize that they're trying to draw her in."

"So?" Marcus watched the women. "I'm curious to see how she'll react."

"Me, too," Bray said. "Maybe they can accomplish what Ford couldn't."

Yeah, Ford was a little curious about that himself.

"They're all terrific, you know." Leaning in, Lucy said, sotto voce, "Ford and Knox were 'men of honor' at my wedding. Like bridesmaids, but male."

Grinning, Skye finally flashed him a glance but quickly looked away. "That sounds like fun."

"It was," Lucy said fondly. "They're my family now."

Karen added, "She and Marcus were fighting the inevitable, but that could only last so long."

"Look who's talking." Lucy added. "Not that Bray was fighting it. Only Karen."

"When a weird ex came after me, I had to ask Bray for help. Turned out that was the smartest move I could have made."

Even from the distance of his own yard, Ford saw Skye's face heating. "Oh, um . . ."

In awe, Ford muttered, "They're sharing their entire histories."

Unconcerned, Marcus shrugged. "They're encouraging her."

"It's been like . . . three minutes." And now Skye knew everything of importance. Well, almost everything.

Lucy, who was always wonderful, didn't give Skye a chance to retreat. "Your plants are beautiful."

Karen asked, "Is that a potted orange tree?"

"It is, and it has fruit. Do you want to see?" Together, they meandered over to Skye's property.

Watching them, Ford said, "Huh." They'd just made that all seem so easy.

A second later, Knox stood. "I want to see the oranges, too." And right behind him, Marcus and Bray said in unison, "I'll go with you."

Together, they bounded down the steps, leaving Ford sitting there alone on the deck.

Damn it. He hadn't gotten new patio furniture just to watch everyone abandon him for his neighbor's house. With a disgusted sigh, he set aside his drink and got up. His trunks were still damp from a recent swim, his hair messy from drying in the sun. Reflective sunglasses hid his eyes, so he felt certain no one would know his surly mood.

Exactly why he was surly, he couldn't say.

Heading that way, he noticed how Skye greeted the guys with surprise, while studiously avoiding looking at him.

He eyed her shorts, long legs, and the halter top that left her shoulders bare. She really could be a model.

As he got nearer, he heard mention of Bray's dog, Rebel. Then Skye surprised him by saying she was considering getting a dog.

"I've been thinking about it for a while. I have a decent-sized yard and it's a nice neighborhood to take a walk."

Knox said, "It's a great idea. There's a local shelter where I help out. I could take you if you want. I know the place, and the pets."

Practically stomping without knowing why, Ford started to say something—and he stepped on a bee. The hot burn immediately told him he'd been stung. "*Son of a*—" Everyone turned to him as he hopped around in pain.

Knox was the first to reach him, grabbing his arm and steering him to Skye's small patio. "Sit down."

She didn't have chairs, so he lowered his ass onto the concrete as the throbbing in his foot intensified.

Squatting down, Knox said, "Damn, man." He pinched the stinger, flicked it away, and then with a whistle, asked, "Are you allergic to bees?"

"No idea. I don't think I've ever been stung." Ford contorted himself to view the bottom of his foot, then cursed again. Already bright red and swelling impressively, it was something to see. And now that he saw the sting, it hurt even more.

"I'll grab some ice." Skye darted into her house, leaving the door open behind her, and seconds later she came rushing back out with a small plastic bowl of ice. Kneeling, she set the bowl aside and gently held one frozen cube against his foot. "This will help."

Ford stared at the top of her head while she circled the ice over the sting. When he glanced at his friends, he saw them all grinning.

Yeah, he felt like a fool. "It's fine."

"You're definitely allergic," she countered. Lifting the ice, she pressed the backs of her fingers to his foot. "It's already hot. Do you have an antihistamine?"

He grumbled, "I'm a pharmaceutical rep, not a drugstore."

Exasperated, she told Knox, "Keep rubbing the ice on his foot."

"Yes, ma'am."

Back in the house she went.

Knox attempted to do as ordered, but Ford didn't let him.

"Give me that." He could damn well ice his own foot.

Rushing back out again, Skye held two pill bottles in one hand and a cola in the other. "Here, an antihistamine and pain pills."

Appalled, Ford pulled back. "I don't need those." Sure, he had pain, but it wasn't all that. He didn't want everyone standing around fussing over him.

Lucy bent down to peer at his foot, then winced. "Take the meds, Ford, or your foot will be too swollen for you to walk."

Patting his shoulder, Karen offered encouragement. "They'll help, I promise."

Rolling his eyes, he said, "It's only a bee sting."

Skye deftly popped out the pills and lifted them to his mouth. "Stop being a baby."

Unbelievable.

Mocking him, Marcus said, "Stop being a baby, Ford," in a ridiculous voice.

"Here." Knox took one of the pills, and then pretended to fly it toward his mouth . . . the way a mother might do with a toddler she was feeding. "Open up so the plane can land."

"Swear to God, Knox, I'm going to punch you."

Chuckling, Knox said, "You're stressing out the ladies. Just take your medicine, already."

Bray crossed his massive arms. "I could hold him while you jam them down his throat. Had to do that with Rebel once when he needed meds. Poor dog hated me for an hour."

Ford narrowed his eyes. "I would hate you for *life*." Huffing, he stuck out his open palm in silent demand.

Skye glanced at everyone, bit her lip to hold back a grin, and gave him the pills.

After tossing them back, he took a drink of cola to wash them down. "Is everyone happy now?" Without waiting for an answer, he got to his feet, or rather foot, and—hobbling—started back to his place. Silence reigned behind him. Not the good kind, but the kind that spelled either trouble or uproarious laughter.

Knowing his friends as he did, he figured on the latter.

Remembering what he'd heard right before getting stung, he turned back and said to Skye, "A dog is a good idea. When do you want to go to the shelter? *I'll* take you."

Put on the spot, she stood, too, then needlessly dusted off her backside and stalled.

Ford said, "I'm off at four tomorrow."

"Shelter closes at six," Knox offered.

She drew a deep breath, curved her mouth in a tight smile, and said, "That should give us enough time to see the dogs."

Something dangerously close to relief loosened Ford's chest. He nodded. "I'll pick you up at four fifteen." Then, keeping as much dignity intact as he could and keenly eyeing the grass for more bees, he limped back to his own house. Odd as it all seemed, progress had been made.

Progress to what though? That's what he didn't know.

It shouldn't matter, yet Skye stared in the mirror, studying her reflection, seeing all the flaws, and taking extra time to try to disguise them. Concealer, contour shadow, the right application of blusher ... Blowing out a breath, she knew it didn't matter.

Ford shouldn't matter.

Damn it, he was a neighbor, maybe a bit of a friend now, and he was her wingman. Period. Nothing more than that.

He'd come to the task grudgingly, so she wouldn't do a single thing to make it more difficult for him.

Such as admire him. Like him. *Want* him.

She groaned. Wanting guys had never quite worked out for her. She wasn't just twice burned. She was like ... five times burned. It sucked.

Her self-esteem had taken a beating, but the desire remained. And why not? She was only twenty-five, healthy, strong and fit.

Sure, she could have a random hookup, but that wasn't for her.

Clyde would have been so willing, but oh no, her fickle heart hadn't been interested. That would have been too easy, and she knew by now that somehow, someway, everything was more complicated for her.

When the knock sounded on her door, she froze. He was early.

Fifteen blasted minutes early!

Quickly she fluffed her hair again, pulling forward several long tresses, dragged in a breath, and headed to the living room. Clyde's persistence prompted her to peek out the window before opening the door.

Well, crap. Worse than Clyde. Worse than Ford jumping the gun.

Aggrieved, she jerked open the door and said, "What are you doing here?"

Laylee, her younger twin by minutes, pressed her way in

with a giant smile and an exuberant hug. "Surprise, Skye. I'm taking you to dinner."

"Dinner?"

"Yup. You're free, and now I'm free, so—"

"Um, see, the thing is . . ."

"Ugh." Laylee held Skye back so she'd get the full brunt of her frown. "Do *not* tell me you're back to seeing Clyde."

"Nope. I ended that." And she was doing her best to ensure he was out of her life for good.

"Thank God. He was all wrong for you." Grabbing Skye's arm and dragging her to the sofa before she could even close the door, Laylee asked, "How did he take it?" As if to offer sympathy and support, she gripped Skye's hands. "I'm sure he was a complete and total jerk, wasn't he? I only had to meet Clyde to know it. Strange that you didn't realize it sooner."

"So strange," Skye said, maybe with a touch of irony. After all, Laylee was the reason Skye had discovered what a jerk Clyde was.

"I'm glad he's out of the picture. Now you'll have more time for me. I'm brokenhearted, you know." Her grin belied that statement.

"Oh, sure," Skye said. "I can see the tears welling up."

Laylee laughed. "Well, I should be brokenhearted. Dejected. Forlorn. I'm just not sure I have it in me."

"Why should you be . . . all that?"

"I got ditched. Can you believe it? *Me.*"

"Incredible." Her sister was nothing if not vain. Then again, why shouldn't Laylee recognize her own beauty? Unlike Skye, she didn't have a single flaw. The bridge of her nose was not a little too wide. Her lips were not too full. Her ears were dainty. Her brows finely arched.

Compared to Laylee, Skye looked like a troglodyte. The missing link. A direct descendent of a cave dweller. "What fool would do such a thing?"

Waving the question off as unimportant, Laylee said, "Men can't take a straightforward woman. Cowards, all of them."

Hmm. Her sister liked to come on strong and fast, pretty much the opposite of Skye, and it often intimidated people. Not that Laylee had ever been serious about a man. She was a serial dater who liked a lot of variety. Again, the opposite of Skye.

"I'm glad you're single again," Laylee said, "because now we can be single together. We'll have so much fun. I know all the best places to find the finest guys."

And therein was one of the reasons Clyde had come in handy. Skye didn't like the singles scene. "You know I'm not a partier, and I have zero interest in casual hookups."

"Meaning you have zero interest in sex?"

With the right guy, she did, but she'd never been able to convince her sister of that.

"Skye," her sister wailed. "I know that look!"

Wrinkling her nose, Skye admitted, "Far as I can tell, sex is overrated."

"Oh, honey." Her tone rich with sympathy, Laylee said, "You're always picking the wrong guys."

Every guy she'd ever "picked" had been at Laylee's suggestion, but Skye refrained from pointing that out. "I have other, more important priorities right now."

"Ugh, you're talking about your house again, aren't you? What is it now? New furniture? New flooring?" Pretending to gag, Laylee asked, "New *drapes*?"

"I think I'd like a pool." Seeing Ford's had inspired her. How nice would it be to float out there on the cool water under the sunshine, maybe with a frosty drink nearby? She could float her troubles away.

"No." Laylee sat forward. "Enough with the homemaker routine. Next you'll be adopting five cats and knitting cardigans. You're *young*, and that means *I'm* young. Let's go out and have fun. Let's burn up the town. I promise I'll find you a guy to rock your world, and then you'll see what I mean."

Sometimes her sister had a one-track mind. "I'll get us something to drink." Fleeing the couch and darting into the kitchen, Skye wondered how to handle the situation. She and Laylee were close—twins were like that. More so than anyone else, she understood her sister. She saw Laylee's vulnerabilities, which, granted, weren't easy to spot in someone so vibrant, outgoing, and assertive.

Growing up with constant comparisons to her more sociable twin had worn down Skye's confidence. She knew it, but conquering her insecurity wasn't easy.

Laylee had been the favored twin, Miss Perfection, always admired for her beauty and style, but in many ways, Laylee had found that a difficult standard to bear.

For much of their lives, Skye had worked doubly hard to compensate for her shortcomings, while Laylee had sought a way to shatter illusions of perfection.

Overall, Skye thought they each just wanted to be accepted for who they were, faults and all.

She was stepping back into the room with two colas when Ford glanced around the open door and said, "Knock, knock."

It took a mere second for Skye to know he'd listened in.

Oh, dear God.

His beautiful green eyes first settled on Skye, and his mouth did this sexy little trick of not quite smiling, yet somehow conveying reassurance, as if to say, "Everything is fine." Then his gaze shifted to Laylee, and he cocked one eyebrow.

Gaze back to Skye. Back to Laylee. On Skye again as he said, "I didn't realize you were a twin."

She hadn't moved. Actually, neither had Laylee. They both just stared at him.

No one would ever accuse Ford of being shy, so he stepped

on in, closed the door, and leaned against it, arms folded. Waiting.

And yes, he looked *very* fine standing there.

Skye got it together first. "Yes," she said, trepidation making her smile sickly. "Though you can see that we aren't identical."

"Close enough." Looking only at Skye, he lowered his voice. "Sorry for intruding."

Because he didn't blink, she didn't either. "Ah, um, it's fine." Condensation from the colas started to drip over her fingers. "How's your foot?"

"You could be a nurse. The ice and the antihistamine did the trick."

"Not tender?"

"Only a little. I can walk." His sexy mouth curved a tiny bit more. "Are we still on for the shelter?"

The shelter. *How did I forget?* Her sister had always had a way of throwing her off-balance. "Yes." Determined now, she stepped to the coffee table and set each drink on a coaster. "Laylee just stopped in, but we won't be long."

His gaze moved over her face as if he'd never seen her before. Still in that low, gentle tone, he asked, "Would you rather I come back? We can spare a few minutes."

"No, it's fine." Somehow she'd make it so, despite her humiliation. Speaking of that . . . With a hard nudge, she tried to disrupt Laylee's gawking.

Didn't work.

No wonder, considering the force of Ford's presence. The man entered a room and all the air turned thick and steamy. She still recalled the first time she'd seen him in his yard. Tall, with a hard, fit physique, dark blond hair, devilish green eyes, and a smile that could weaken a woman's knees. Confidence. Amusement.

Interest.

He had it all. She loudly cleared her throat, desperate to break the tension. "Laylee, this is my neighbor, Ford Caruso. He's going with me to a shelter to pick out a dog." *Not* a cat, though she wouldn't mind a cat, too, eventually.

At least cardigans were nowhere on the horizon.

Laylee being Laylee, she put a hand to her throat and hummed suggestively. "You have this specimen living next door and you've never introduced me?"

Ford grinned. "Until recently, we hadn't been close." He strode in and held out a hand. "Nice to meet you."

Heart deflating, Skye waited for the new romance to begin. Her sister won over men *so* easily . . . even the men that interested Skye. It had been happening since before high school. For Laylee, winning over a guy was as easy as picking wildflowers. She always knew what to say, when to say it, and her boldness was only topped by her devastating looks.

If she wasn't Laylee's sister, Skye probably wouldn't like her on principle alone.

Ford had a difficult time taking in everything he was noticing. Not just the twin, who enjoyed being outrageous, but the way Skye retreated, emotionally if not physically.

There was a touch of jealousy—each of the other, though he doubted Skye realized that her sister envied her. Laylee, who was a more delicate version of Skye, probably needed her sister a lot. For many things.

What he'd heard . . . No, if he thought about that too much, he'd end up offering to show Skye a few more positive experiences. That wasn't on the agenda though—she'd made that clear—and now more than ever, he wanted to be available to her.

As a friend. A fake significant other to fend off interest. And as protection if she needed it.

It was a novel experience, and he wasn't sure he liked it. As with most medicine, it didn't taste great but was probably good for his character.

He squeezed in next to Skye on the couch, and she gave him a look of surprise. "So, have you thought about what type of dog you want?"

With him so close, she turned her head and stared at him.

He grinned. *That's right*, he thought. *I won't ask about your sexual misadventures, so relax.* What he'd overheard was her own private business. She could discuss it with him or not, but he wouldn't put her on the spot.

"I . . ."

"Small, large?"

She pursed her lips. "I guess small and cute would be best. Easier to take care of and all that."

"A yapper," he said with a nod. "They're notorious heel nippers."

Her worry eased and she smiled. "You sound like a man familiar with small dogs."

"A few. They can be really territorial." Especially with women. "Disgruntled pooches have a knack for trying to ruin my plans with dates."

Skye laughed, but Laylee murmured, "I bet you don't let much get in your way."

Ignoring that, he said, "If I got a dog, it'd be something muscular. Friendly but capable." Envisioning one particular dog would only frustrate him. He was used to wanting things he couldn't or shouldn't get. That feeling of disappointment reminded him of his youth and all the high expectations he'd had for his life. "A dog who'd chase a ball or a Frisbee. Who'd enjoy a jog, and a ride in the car with the window open."

In the softest voice he'd ever heard from her, Skye said, "That does sound nice. Do you have a dog in mind?"

"She doesn't need a *dog*." Tired of being left out, Laylee

leaned forward to peer around her sister, and when that didn't suffice, she moved to the chair to take center stage. "She needs a man."

"I'm a man," he said, holding out his arms. "I don't think she needs another. But a dog? Everyone needs a dog."

"Then why don't you have one?" Laylee asked.

"One day I will." If the dog he wanted was still available. Rather than get too introspective, he shook his head. "Maybe when I settle down and all that."

Skye said low, "In a hundred years or so?"

He teased back, "Exactly." In truth, he hoped it wouldn't take that long.

Laylee crossed her legs. "So you two are . . . ?"

Skye went comically still. Probably her usual reaction to her outrageous sister's nosiness.

No problem for him though. He stroked two fingers along a lock of Skye's hair, down her cheek, over her shoulder.

He heard her small, sharp inhalation.

God, her hair was silky, and so pretty. She wore it a little darker than Laylee's, but with a few select highlights that framed her face. A face that was a little rounder than her sister's, and softer because of it. Darker brows, too, which made them more noticeable. And those plump lips . . . They were a focal point on her face, at least for him.

Settling his hand on her knee, he gave a smile of pure seduction. It usually worked, and seeing the flare of heat in Skye's eyes, he knew he still had it. "Now, Laylee," he said, without taking his gaze from Skye's midnight eyes. "I'm guessing a woman like you doesn't need it spelled out."

In a cunning tone, she repeated, "A woman like me?"

Making his expression as bland as he could, Ford glanced at her. Oh, this one was good at getting her way in most situations. "You're Skye's sister, so I assumed you were as astute as she is . . . but maybe not?"

Skye took another quick breath, this time more of a gasp. "We should go." Abruptly, she shot to her feet. "We don't want the shelter to close on us."

More slowly, Ford rose, too.

Laylee watched them both. "Are you set up for a dog? A bed, treats, dishes, food?"

Skye bit her lip. "No. I wasn't sure what to get."

"You have time," Ford assured her. "They won't give you the dog today. You'll just choose the one you want, then fill out an application. It's their way of ensuring the animals go to a good home."

She released a breath. "Oh, good. So I'll put that on my agenda for tomorrow."

He opened his mouth, and Laylee said, "Great idea. We can shop together. Maybe after lunch."

Almost wincing, Skye turned to her sister. "You're coming back tomorrow?"

"Actually"—she bounced her gaze back and forth between them, then gave a sly grin—"I think I'll spend the night."

Ha! Did she hope to disrupt her sister's plans? He admired her persistence. "No problem. I mean, I live right next door." His grin was no less sly than hers. "Plenty of privacy to go around."

"Here." Skye shoved her cola into his hand. "You can have it. I need to speak to Laylee just a moment."

He sipped the cold drink. "Should I wait next door?"

"No need." Laylee finally stood, then smoothed her body-hugging dress, making a point of stroking her hands over her waist, hips, and derriere. "We can talk when she gets home tonight."

Ford knew exactly what she wanted, but he didn't oblige her. After a mere glance, he gave his attention back to Skye. "Does that work for you?"

Without waiting for her sister to reply, Laylee said, "I'll get my overnight bag out of the car."

Skye practically locked her jaw. "Fine. Make yourself at home."

"Don't I always?"

The second she stepped outside, Ford chuckled. "I always wanted a sibling. These types of shenanigans seem fun—at least from the outside looking in."

Surprised, Skye looked up at him, a load of curiosity in her eyes. "You really think so?"

"Definitely." She needed to know that her sister wasn't a problem for him, not in any way.

"Usually Laylee comes on so strong that she . . ." The words tapered off.

"Scares people off? Offends? Draws all the attention?" It amused him. "That seemed to be her plan. I imagine it was tough, having a twin so different from you."

Allegiance had her saying, "Laylee can be overwhelming, and we're different in a lot of ways, but she's always there for me."

Just as he'd suspected. "Family. That's how it should be, right?" As if he had a clue. "Being an only child sucked, at least most of the time."

Three seconds ticked by as her gaze delved into his, possibly seeing things he didn't want to show. Her tone was sweet and caring when she asked, "But not always?"

"I couldn't have left home when I did if I'd had a little brother or sister." He was often a dick, but he was loyal—to those who deserved loyalty.

His parents hadn't.

Getting himself back on track, he said, "By the way, you look amazing."

As if she'd forgotten what she wore, she glanced down at her tailored white shorts, tan tank top, and brown leather sandals. "I wasn't sure about the white, since we'll be seeing animals, but I didn't know—" Before she could finish that thought, her sister breezed back in with a large purple tote overflowing with toiletries, and a small floral suitcase.

"Skye looks prettier in bold colors, but she rarely wears them."

"She's so stunning in natural shades, why would she? Believe me, she doesn't need to draw more attention." The fact that Laylee's dress was brightly colored hadn't slipped his notice. "I vote she leaves the bold colors to you." The compliment had both women studying him, Skye in flustered confusion and Laylee with uncertain affront. He'd been vague enough that neither of them knew if he'd complimented or insulted Laylee.

It was almost laughable. Almost.

Playing his part—or so he told himself—he stroked Skye's hair again and looked into her beautiful eyes. "Although I'm sure you're stunning whatever you wear . . . or don't wear."

Her eyes flared wide and stayed that way. Laylee looked equally surprised.

Satisfied with those reactions, he asked Skye, "Do you have everything you need?"

She instinctively glanced around, then with an, "Oh," she grabbed up her purse from the console. "Ready."

He took her hand. "Catch you later, Laylee." The silence was damning, but he didn't mind. In fact, he came close to grinning.

It helped that Laylee suddenly laughed and leaned out the door behind them. "I like him, Skye! He's slick, but funny, and almost perfect."

Nice to hear her sister wish her well. At least, he thought that was what she'd done. Skye didn't look overly certain about her sister's intention either.

Once they were on their way, the silence stretched out. He glanced at her. "Are we going to talk about it?"

"What?"

"Your amusing sister."

Low, she muttered, "I don't think she was trying to be amusing."

No, probably not. At least not at first. "Does she do that often?"

This time with her jaw tight, she repeated, "What?"

Damn, their reactions were both funny. "Try to steal the show."

"There's no *try* to it. Laylee gets the lion's share of attention just by existing."

Not how he saw it, but trying to imagine it from her point of view, he understood. "Maybe because the second she shows up, you retreat. Don't think I didn't notice." Even with his gaze on the road, he felt the keen attention his words got.

"You think I retreated?"

"Seriously? You gave her the stage." He expected her to deny it, but instead she pondered.

"Maybe I do. Habit from long ago and all that."

It wasn't until they were approaching the shelter that she spoke again. "You have a beautiful car."

"Thanks." He glanced around the interior of his Mercedes. "You know, I'd prefer a kickass truck like Knox's, but being a pharmaceutical rep means looking the part."

Her brows twitched together. "You can't just drive whatever you want?" Before he could answer, she twisted in her seat to partially face him. "I'm curious about your job. You seem to have odd hours."

Aha. He tried not to gloat, but it wasn't easy. "I thought you didn't make note of my comings and goings."

"With women," she specified. "I have noticed that sometimes you're home more, and other times you're gone all day."

"My schedule changes a lot. I'm usually up by six, and by seven I'm either making calls from home or heading out to medical offices or hospitals to meet with doctors before they start seeing patients. Probably half my day is spent traveling to meetings with physicians, pharmacists, staff, or other clients. I can usually sneak in an hour or two of gym time, and when I can't, I jog when I get home."

"Or swim laps in your pool."

Another aha. "Noticed that, too, did you?"

"Don't act like I'm spying on you." She fought a grin. "There's not a lot of distance between our houses. When I'm home and the windows are open, I hear you splashing."

She made him sound like a kid. Oddly, he didn't mind that. "Swimming is a nice switch to my routine, at least in the summer. Not so much in the fall, winter, or spring." To wrap it up, he explained, "I usually bring my lunch to a doctor's office. It gives me a chance to share drug samples and product brochures. Around all that I make more calls, either to set up meetings, or chat with my manager to discuss strategies."

"Wow, you're busy."

Unsure what to make of that observation, he shrugged. "I'm often a sales leader at the company." Often enough to irk others and to get ribbed by his friends for being an overachiever. With a quick frown, he wondered if he should have mentioned it. Did it sound like bragging?

When she said nothing, he tried to correct any false assumptions. "I'm competitive, but I don't mind when someone else takes the spot." Not much, anyway. "I've helped some of the others with ideas or given them some leads when I need a little more free time."

As if she didn't understand what a sacrifice that was, she teased. "Free time for women."

It struck him that she was right, but not the way she meant. He had freed up time, but not always for dating. "I meant time for friends, and some of them are women . . . like Lucy. She's just one of the guys."

"She said that to me."

"It's true. We all like sports, and so does she, but we're really into MMA. That's Bray's sport, and he's good."

Interested, she angled toward him. "I've never watched it, but it sounds fascinating."

"Lucy could tell you all about it. She's this awesome mix of knowledgeable sports fan, competitor, and homemaker."

"I can see why you enjoy spending time with her."

He'd given up leads to hang out with his friends. "Lucy adds something to the mix. Great female company with all the perks—minus anything sexual." Smile going crooked, he admitted, "It's something of a novel experience for me."

Instead of laughing with him, she grew serious. "You said you don't have siblings, but what about other female relatives? Like an aunt or cousin?"

No relatives at all. It'd be weirdly uncomfortable to admit that though, so he only shook his head. "None that I know of."

"Well, sounds to me like your friends are the same as family, only better."

"You think?" He didn't know enough about real family to make the judgment. To his heart though, Marcus, Bray, and Knox were his brothers.

"Sure. All the fun and none of the baggage."

Did Skye have a lot of baggage with her family? "We all get together for the televised fights, and Lucy always brings something to eat. Good stuff, like really filling finger food and homemade cookies."

"Ah, so she won you over with food."

Being honest, he said, "It was everything about her, really. She fit with us, you know? For a while, she and Marcus tried to pretend they were only friends." A few memories had him grinning. "Right up until Marcus couldn't take it. It was fun to watch them explode."

"Explode?"

"Go all hot and heavy on each other. To tease him, we each pretended to get closer to her, too. Poor Lucy didn't know what to think." Remembering Lucy's background, he sobered. "She had a rough start in life, but now she's as happy as anyone can be."

Not bothering to hide her fascination, Skye asked, "And Karen?"

"She had a super-creepy stalker." Karen had always been private about her experience, so usually he wouldn't have mentioned it. He was still surprised that she'd told Skye. "When she asked Bray for help, she found out that he'd do anything for her. He already loved her. All he'd needed was an opening to show it."

Skye sighed dramatically. "They seem really happy now."

"They are." Marcus and Bray had the forever kind of marriages. He was glad for them—and he envied their contentment.

After a brief hesitation, she asked, "Did it change the dynamic of your group? Marcus and Bray getting married, I mean."

"A little. Lucy was already a part of things, but she wasn't a wife. I guess we treated her a little different after their marriage." He thought about it and grinned. "Not much though."

"Good. I don't think she'd want any of you to change."

"Probably not. Karen was a little more reserved, definitely quieter than the rest of us." She was warming up to them though, little by little, letting down her guard. "We get together less often now, but it's okay because sometimes there are six of us, and sometimes it's just Knox and me."

"Ford and Knox," she mused aloud. "Makes me think of Fort Knox."

"If you tell Knox that, he'll probably have shirts made, just to irk me."

When she laughed, he warned, "I'll give you mine in front of him, then *you'll* have to wear it."

She pretended to wipe off her smile, but it remained, teasing those delectable lips of hers.

They had almost reached the shelter and so far, he'd done the majority of the talking. "What about you? What's your job description?"

"I'm a merchandiser."

The way she said it, he could tell she didn't expect questions. "And that means . . . ?"

"Well, I used to work for a big department store chain, but that involved a lot of travel to trade shows and stuff, and I guess at heart I'm a homebody."

A homebody sounded nice. "Like Lucy."

"Minus the cooking skill. I can get by. Clearly, I'm not going hungry, right?"

*Nope*, he told himself. *Resist glancing at her body. Keep your eyes on the road.* "You look healthy, if that's what you mean."

She laughed. "I cook the basics, but I won't be tempting hordes of hungry men anytime soon."

Oh, he didn't know about that. "Not sure you'd need culinary skill to do that." *Shit.* Probably shouldn't have said that, but it was hard to fight his natural instincts.

Surprise, and then puzzled pleasure showed on her face. "Thank you."

*Concentrate on your driving.* The seconds ticked by, not really uncomfortable, but still . . . "I can cook." He said it, then wondered if it sounded like more bragging. "Basics, I mean. Working the grill. Breakfast. That sort of thing."

"Same. Living alone, there's not a lot of reason for a complicated meal."

"Guess not." And damn it, didn't that sound lonely? For him at least. She didn't seem lonely at all. "Do you miss big home-cooked meals?"

"Sometimes. Pot roast with potatoes and carrots." She hummed a sound of appreciation. "Fried chicken. A pot of chili.

Some meals are just better homemade. Luckily, close to where I work now, there's a little family-owned restaurant that serves traditional dinners."

She was making him hungry—and not just for food. "So you switched jobs?"

"After I bought the house, I took a position with Helen's Boutiques."

"That's a little ritzy place downtown, right?"

She nodded. "The first store was opened by Helen Montgomery, who was great-grandmother to the current owners. They have six stores now, all in the tristate area, Ohio, Northern Kentucky, and parts of Indiana, all run by family members. Luckily, I only have to do serious travel a few times a year. It helps that a lot of the buying is done online now. The trade shows are still helpful so I can see the quality and fit of some pieces." Lacking enthusiasm, she said, "I have to watch a lot of fashion shows to see what's up-and-coming. Not all of it works for a rural area like ours, but colors and patterns can trend everywhere."

"You have great style, so I'm sure that work is a perfect fit for you."

Again, she appeared nonplussed by the compliment. "I'm actually considered the unfashionable one in my family. Most of my relatives favor striking colors."

"And you'd rather blend in?"

"Something like that."

Not that she ever could. The understated colors and casual vibe of her clothes only made her more appealing. "Being different is good." He was certainly different from his parents.

He wondered what her fashionable sister did, but refused to ask. He had a feeling that Skye expected him to, that she thought he'd be more interested in Laylee than in her. Not a chance. He knew plenty of women like Laylee.

Not sure he'd ever met anyone like Skye.

"We're here." He pulled into the shelter, aware of her leaning forward to look out the windshield in excitement. She had a beautiful profile—and he was pretty sure her long hair would be factoring into a few fantasies for him. "Ready?"

Nodding, she opened her door and stepped out. A couple of dogs were in the right-side yard with volunteers, others in enclosed runs on the opposite side.

Her gaze bounced around everywhere. "Is it silly that I'm nervous?"

"Not silly at all." Drawn to her, he put a hand to the small of her back and guided her in. "I've been here before. Did I tell you that?"

She stopped to stare at him. "You have?"

"Knox told you he volunteers here."

Her smile slipped into place. "And where he goes, you go?"

"Something like that." Knox was often a good influence. "When they were training new volunteers, I joined in, but I don't have time to take part often." And he felt guilty as hell about it. "Sometimes it feels like I spend so much time working—driving, meeting, and making calls—that I barely have time to keep up with the guys."

"That's why you don't mind that Marcus and Bray married."

He laughed. "Minding wouldn't have done me much good, not the way they feel about their wives, but the truth is, I'm happy for them. Like you said, for me they're family." For the others, getting together and staying in touch might not be such a big deal. Knox had a doting mom and dad that he was close to. Marcus had his adoptive parents, and now Lucy. Bray had not only his adoptive parents and Karen, but his impressive fight family, too.

In comparison, Ford didn't have . . . anyone.

The important people in his life were associated with his friends. *Their* families. *Their* wives.

He couldn't claim to miss his mother and father. Even when he'd lived with them, they'd been nothing more than strangers existing under the same roof. What he missed was the idea of them. Of having roots. Someone who would think of him and worry a little.

And care.

Someone to include him in a home-cooked meal.

"Ford." Skye touched her fingertips to his upper arm. "I was only teasing. I know you're happy for them. I can see how close you all are."

# Chapter 3

What. The. Hell. He'd been so completely lost in thought, he hadn't noticed when Skye quit looking at the shelter and instead stared at him.

What was it about her that had him thinking deep thoughts? Whatever had brought it on, he'd end it right now.

The cocky grin came automatically as he quickly covered. "I'm fine. I was just thinking of a dog that would be perfect for you." He led her through two sets of doors that ensured no animals got out. Cats often wandered the lobby, greeting everyone who came in. "Thing is, he's bonded to another beast of a dog, and I'm not sure separating them would be a good idea."

Overwhelmed, she turned in a circle to take in the giant glass-fronted room full of playful kittens. There was a supply area for anyone who forgot the necessities when picking up their pet, and several cat towers, most with older cats stationed on them in one lazy pose or another. "This is . . . wow. I can hear the dogs, but I don't see them."

"They're through there." He indicated the hall, but waited

until Nikki, the harried front desk manager, finished a call, then rushed over to them. "Ford, hi."

"Hi, Nikki." He accepted a squeezing hug from the fifty-something woman. She was tall and wiry, with short, spiky, flame-colored hair and a zest for life that encompassed not only animals, but humans, too. Ford liked her a lot. "How's it going?"

"Busy! We've had a terrific adoption month." Eyeing Skye with open curiosity, she offered, "Maybelline is still here though. Did you want to visit her?"

The name amused him. "That's sticking, huh?"

"Of course it is. It's perfect for her." She said to Skye, "The first time Ford saw Maybelline, he named her, because he said no amount of cosmetics would help. She's a sweetheart, but not the prettiest dog we've ever taken in. She sure does adore Ford." As if imparting a secret, she leaned in and whispered, "He adores her right back."

"Aww," Skye said, gazing at him with new, softer emotions.

He couldn't take it. "Since I'm here, I might as well check in on her." He nodded to Skye. "This is my neighbor, Skye Fairchild. She's interested in adopting. Maybe while you get her info, I could sit with Maybelline."

"She'll be thrilled to see you." Nikki led Skye to a chair in front of her desk and handed her a form. "Go ahead and get started on that and I'll be right back."

Ford saw the way Skye concentrated on the questions, her expression so earnest that his heart clenched a little at the sight of her.

As they walked away, he said to Nikki, "She'll be an incredible pet owner."

"You said she's a neighbor?"

"Right next door." Because Nikki knew him well, he promised, "I'll keep an eye on things, too. If she needs any help, I'm there."

Nikki smiled. "Doesn't sound like she's just a neighbor."

There was nothing *just* about Skye Fairchild. The more he knew, the more he wanted to know. Hopefully, that wouldn't become a problem.

Fishing, Nikki said, "She's gorgeous, too."

"Very." Though Skye honestly didn't seem to realize it.

Beyond them, the most godawful racket started, making Ford smile. Apparently, Maybelline had heard him talking. "I'm coming," he said in a singsong voice, and the frantic howling increased.

Laughing, Nikki turned the corner with him and there she was. Maybelline, all one hundred pounds of her.

Slinging drool and dancing around on her giant paws, the dog looked as if a St. Bernard and Bigfoot had gotten together. Big, muscular, with a massive head, a few scars, and at present, a look of love in her eyes.

Seeing him, she gave a loud *woof* that shook the walls.

Because he loved her intelligence, he said, "Shh," just to see one of her better tricks.

The bark changed to a low grumble deep in her throat, like an elderly person mumbling.

"Such a good girl." Forgetting about Nikki for a moment, he said, "Maybelline, no female has ever loved me the way you do."

Snorting at that bit of nonsense, Nikki thwacked him on the shoulder. "I find that hard to believe."

"It's true." Dates had mentioned love before, but it wasn't like this. It wasn't trust and friendship, and a need for a lifetime together.

"You know you want her. Quit fighting the inevitable." Nikki opened the kennel door and clipped a leash to Maybelline's collar. With her big butt going in one direction and her head and shoulders in another, the dog wagged her whole body while plowing out to see him.

She was large enough that Ford didn't have to bend far to hug her, to repeatedly pet her head and neck, whispering soft words to her.

One day he would promise to keep her. How that'd work with his hours, he didn't know, but if he could figure out a way, he would.

When Nikki said, "If you want to take her out, you can," the dog nearly yanked him off his feet, lunging to the kennel next door to hers.

"I take that as a yes."

"But she wants her friend," Nikki pointed out with a grin.

"A sentiment that's obviously shared." High pitched yapping began as a much smaller dog, no more than eight pounds, spun in circles of excitement. A Chihuahua-terrier mix, he wasn't much bigger than Maybelline's paw, yet somehow they'd become besties.

God, he loved animals. If he had the means, he'd adopt a houseful of them. "Can I get a twofer, Nikki?"

"Shoot, yeah. If you didn't let them out together, there'd be no end to the racket." Because the smaller dog was sneakier than Maybelline, Nikki ducked into the kennel to attach the leash before opening the door so the wee one could join Maybelline.

It was hilarious to watch them together. "The odd couple," Ford said, seeing the tiny pooch jump repeatedly to reach Maybelline, only to have Maybelline run her big tongue from one end of the little dog to the other, almost toppling him over. "I'll take them out to the yard for a while. Let me know if Skye needs me."

"I'll bring her to you as soon as she's done."

Nodding, he used a back door to access a fenced area. Volunteers were in the side yards, where trails made it easier to teach the animals the etiquette of being walked, but back here, it was quiet with no one else around.

Maybelline was much calmer now, shortening her long strides so the smaller dog, running, could keep up. Every so often they paused to cuddle and smooch.

Honest to God, his heart was taking a battering today.

Situated beneath a shade tree was one of four picnic tables that Knox had built and donated. Hell of a guy, his buddy Knox. The man could build or repair anything, and often treated work like a vacation. He enjoyed everything he did. Ford envied him that ability.

After he took a seat, Maybelline rested her massive head over his thighs. For such a big, strong girl, she was the gentlest of creatures, and incredibly loving. She deserved a family. She probably deserved someone better than he.

So far, no one had taken her.

People looked at her and saw all the wrong things. They didn't see her enormous capacity for love. Her sweet nature.

Her vulnerability. Her need.

And why the hell was he suddenly feeling so maudlin?

"Come on, pooch." He patted the bench beside him, and the smaller dog jumped up, gaining access to Maybelline's face.

Which he licked. And licked.

*And licked.*

"It's getting a little gross, dude."

Disagreeing, Maybelline sighed in bliss, closing her big brown eyes and accepting all the affection, both from him and the little dog.

"You two are quite the pair. What are we going to do when someone separates you?" He hated that thought so damn much. When you found someone you loved, who loved you back, you shouldn't let them go. Ever.

Didn't matter if they matched or made up the oddest pair ever.

"If only I was home a little more."

Maybelline did that deep rumbling thing that sounded like a

cross between a blender full of rocks and a cat purr. If the cat was a pissed-off lion.

"You'd like my friends." Pretty sure they'd love Maybelline, too. Rock-solid guys, that's what they were. And the women . . . He really enjoyed having female friends, gaining a new perspective on everything.

Probably what he felt for them was similar to what a brother would feel for a sister. Protective, affectionate, and caring without the slow burn of lust. It was comfortable.

Stroking the dog's neck, softly playing with her ears, Ford imagined doing this every night. Maybelline would greet him when he got home from work. They'd have dinner, take a nice long walk, maybe a swim. . . . Did dogs swim in pools?

Maybelline would. And if not, she could sprawl on the deck.

Then they'd crash in front of the TV for a movie or something. "You'd take up the better portion of the couch, but I can get a bigger couch, no problem."

The smaller dog made a noise, almost like a warning, and with a half grin of amusement, he stroked the little rat. "You'd both like Rebel, too. He's my friend's dog." Absurd, but his throat got a little tight at the way the rat leaned into his hand. "No one wanted him either, but now he has a great family."

*Stop drawing comparisons*, he ordered himself—and he didn't mean comparisons between the dogs.

"Family isn't everything though. Good friends are the best." As if deciding Ford was okay, the rat got into his lap and half curled around Maybelline's head, then burrowed his face under her loose lip, using it like a blanket. "See, like that." Both dogs appeared content to sit in the sunshine with him, as long as they were together. "You two are damn cute—do you know that?"

What would happen when Knox settled down? After seeing the way Marcus and Bray had embraced the commitment of marriage, he knew it was only a matter of time. They were at that age. The age when a man's thoughts veered away from the latest bar scene to . . . Well, hell. Doing what he was doing right now. Contemplating the future. Putting down serious roots. Understanding what was important in life—and it wasn't the pool in his backyard.

"I always wanted a dog like you. I know, that sounds odd. You're not much of a chick magnet, and pretty sure you've had some rough experiences." He lightly traced a scar on Maybelline's head where the fur would never return.

It filled him with fury. She was a big but gentle animal. However she'd gotten hurt, it was unforgivable. In a quiet whisper, he asked, "Were you a bait dog, baby? God, I'd like to find the bastard who mistreated you."

Maybelline tilted her head just a little to eye him. "You're still beautiful. Don't let anyone tell you otherwise."

She gave an answering grumble, and damn, it felt as if she wanted to reassure him. "Thanks, girl, but I'm fine."

Shifting, she leaned against him more fully, turned her head to better see him, and almost crushed his junk in the bargain.

"Hey, careful around the jewels." Wincing, he adjusted, straightening one leg. And that had both dogs quickly adjusting, too, until he was back in nearly the same position.

The little dog gave him a look of disdain, making him smile. "Yappers are annoying, but I don't mind your yapping because it's usually warranted. I mean, I get it. People can be jerks . . . me included. If I wasn't a jerk, I'd have already stepped up, right?

While he stroked both dogs, his thoughts continued to riot. "I hate the idea of you guys being separated." He bent over them, encompassing them in a hug. "If I had any family to help out . . ." But he didn't. "Knox is busy enough already, and with Marcus and Bray married, I can't impose on them. What if I had a twelve-hour day? I get those, you know."

Unsure whether he was trying to reason with the dogs or himself, Ford continued. "Much as I'd love to take you home, it wouldn't be fair to have you cooped up all day. I'm trying not to be selfish here."

"I don't think you're selfish."

The intrusion of that soft voice jolted all three of them. Ford jerked upright, Maybelline swung her big head around, and the rat went fiercely bonkers. He leapt off the bench, turned two circles, and gave Skye hell.

"How long have you been there?" Yes, his tone reeked of accusation. He'd just had a lengthy, maudlin, *dramatic* conversation with two dogs. He'd thought he was alone, and there she'd stood, daring to eavesdrop. "Why did you sneak up on me?"

"I saw you talking." Dark blue eyes met his, and in their depths he saw amusement, but also sensitivity. "To the dogs."

"And that meant you had to listen in?"

Lifting one shoulder and elevating her chin, she said, "Sort of like you did earlier when I was talking with Laylee."

Unable to refute that, he shut his mouth. But the small dog wasn't appeased by her explanation.

Skye inched in close and took the seat beside him.

Very close.

Their thighs were pressed together.

How did she expect him to keep things platonic if she was going to go thigh-to-thigh with him? Awareness sparked all through his body, sending his thoughts on an erotic free-for-all.

She bumped her shoulder to his. "This little guy isn't happy with my intrusion, either."

"Those are his attack circles," Ford explained. "He's beyond unhappy. He's enraged."

Bending forward, Skye offered her hand, and the yapper pretended to nip her without doing any real damage. "My, you're a fierce one."

"He doesn't like that you overheard our private conversation."

A dimple appeared in her cheek. "I won't apologize." Turning her attention to Maybelline, she again offered her hand. Big mistake. Maybelline's tongue came out to lap from her fingertips to her elbow, leaving behind a trail of slobber.

Ford snickered. "That's what you get."

Hand held away from her body, Skye searched the area, likely hoping for a way to wipe off the drool.

Ford watched her with glee. "Use the grass."

"Ugh." She leaned farther forward to do that, swiping her palm across the lawn and giving him a stellar view of her backside in the process. "You could have warned me."

Took a second for the words to sink in because his attention was firmly fixed on her derriere. "Fat chance, since you didn't warn me."

Now with her hand partially dry, she dug in her purse and found a tissue.

The yapper continued to complain until Ford scooped him up to Maybelline's face again. Both dogs watched Skye, Maybelline with her usual friendliness, the yapper with furious suspicion.

When Skye finished, she stuck the tissue in her pocket, rested her hands in her lap, and smiled at him. "If I hadn't listened, then I wouldn't have come up with such a brilliant solution."

Skye didn't think she'd ever been so touched by a conversation. Hearing Ford share his feelings so openly with the dogs, knowing he was earnest, had her seeing him in a whole new way. A warmer, more affectionate way.

He'd literally had a heart-to-heart with shelter dogs, and his concern for them, his caring, couldn't have been more genuine.

The slick salesman, the gorgeous neighbor, the die-hard

bachelor and overachiever, was actually a kind, compassionate man.

"You're staring at me," he said.

"I'm sure I'm not the first woman to do so." He was so sinfully sexy, looking had never been a problem. "Don't let it spook you."

"I'm not *spooked*." A dull flush colored his cheekbones. Heat of the day—or more likely embarrassment at being found human. "I can tell you're up to something though."

The yapper finally settled down and even let Skye touch him without all the fuss and feigned outrage.

Maybelline, who truly had soulful eyes, dropped her massive head on Ford's lap again, making him grunt with discomfort.

"They're an adorable pair." And there was no way she could walk away from this. From them.

From Ford.

When exactly he'd become more than a neighbor, she didn't know. If he realized the direction of her thoughts, he'd probably drop out as her wingman. He'd get stingy with his smiles again, and she'd be back to square one.

The problem was, now that she knew him better, no one else would do.

"You said you had a solution." Still disgruntled, Ford scowled at her. "Let's hear it, and then I'll decide if it's brilliant."

"We should adopt the dogs."

Alarm shot his brows skyward and had him tilting away from her. "We, as in together?"

The way he choked on the word *together* tickled her. "We're not together, so, no, I didn't mean that. You can relax."

Instead, he seemed more irascible. "What *do* you mean?"

"I'm not proposing, Ford. I'm not even suggesting we be a real couple." Not that she'd mind giving that a try, but it would have to come second to other, more important things. Like two beautiful dogs who definitely needed homes. "I promise, I haven't forgotten our agreement."

He started to say something, changed his mind, and shrugged. "It's your agreement. You can forget it whenever you want."

That left her a little speechless. How did he mean that? That he'd be happy to bail whenever she released him? Or that he might want more than their arranged ruse?

"I'm looking forward to the dinner," he said. "And the party."

She had serious doubts about that but smiled. "Good, because I'm not letting you off the hook."

He smiled, too, and mimicked her with, "Good."

The sunlight made his green eyes even brighter, and when she caught herself leaning toward him, she cleared her throat and refocused on the dogs. "Our yards run together. I'm not planning to move, and I don't think you're planning to move?"

"I'm not."

"So why don't we adopt the dogs." To convince him, she hurried on with her talking points. "I can take this little thug and you can take Maybelline, and when necessary, we can puppy sit for each other. Plus, they could spend time together during the day. My house, or your house, and sometimes in the yard."

Surprise slowly replaced his smile. Pleasant surprise, she hoped. She wasn't quite sure about that yet. He studied her eyes, maybe gauging her seriousness, then looked at Maybelline before asking, "You'd really do that?"

The naked yearning in his tone, in the way he touched the dog, told an entire story, one he wasn't ready to share. Anyone could see that Ford loved the big lug, but he hesitated to take her because he didn't want her to be shortchanged.

There were layers to Ford Caruso that fascinated her. "We'd probably need to get our yards fenced as soon as possible, but once we do, we could add a gate between them so that when the dogs want to visit, they can."

"What happens if you get pissed at me?"

Hearing more than what he'd actually said, she asked, "Why would that happen?"

Expression droll, he shot her the side eye. "We're neighbors. You're a woman." Before she could get riled, he lifted a hand. "I'm a man. People disagree on things."

"Hmm. You could be right. I can imagine a hundred ways you might infuriate me." Given the annoyance in his gaze, teasing him was way too easy. "So let me see if I understand. Your concern is that, when you irk me—and we both assume you will—I'll . . . what? Withhold the dog from you?"

"Or from Maybelline." With gentle commiseration, he traced his fingertips along an old scar on the dog's neck. "She's been hurt enough. Withholding her buddy wouldn't be fair to her."

"No, it wouldn't." The dog gazed adoringly at Ford. "I'd have to be a terrible person to do that, but I'm not. I think I'm nice. Flawed in many ways, but not mean or spiteful."

He nodded his acceptance. "So you know, I'm the same." With a crooked grin, he clarified, "Plenty flawed, but not vindictive."

Her heartbeat was picking up speed with all the possibilities ahead. "She loves you."

He snorted. "She's a dog."

"Yes, and she loves you." Why was that so hard for him to understand? "If it'll make you feel better, you can adopt both dogs. I'll still let this little guy live with me, and I promise to share equally in all the responsibilities, both financially and by helping out with whatever they need." For three seconds, she allowed herself the pleasure of leaning into him. "You can trust me to keep my word for . . . let's say three months. That way if, or when, you decide I'm not the proper sort of pet owner, you'll have all the control."

New interest glowed in his eyes. "I like the idea of having control with you."

Wow. Okay, yeah, heat just scorched her clear down to her toes. Wasn't easy, but she forced a careless smile. "Was that a sexual innuendo? If so, that kind of thing can cause confusion."

The corner of his mouth hitched. "Sorry. It comes naturally."

"I'm sure." He really was slick, making it tough to tell what he genuinely thought and felt. "If you're ever serious, you might have to spell it out for me."

He did a double take, his gaze searching hers. "Fair enough."

The back door of the shelter opened, and Nikki leaned out. "Sorry to break up the visit, but we're closing in fifteen minutes." She looked at each dog, and then, with obvious hope, at Ford and Skye. "So, um, any decisions made?"

Pitching her voice low, Skye said, "I'll even pay to have the yards fenced."

"No, you won't," he said just as low. "And we'll each adopt to keep it fair. I'm trusting you."

Her heartbeat went into overdrive. "I'm trusting you, too."

Somehow, his smile added to his already devastating appeal. He shifted his gaze to Nikki. "We've come up with a solution."

Incredibly happy, Skye said, "I'd like the little ruffian."

"And I'll take Maybelline." He grinned at the dog. "This way, they'll still be able to visit."

Bursting into a loud cheer, Nikki danced out to the yard. "That's incredible! Such great news!" She twirled, which got Maybelline and the little dog doing the same.

Ford laughed, and because the excitement was contagious, he caught Skye's hands and pulled her up to dance her around the yard, too.

The reason didn't matter; she liked seeing him so happy.

She also liked touching him.

Huh. When was the last time that had happened to her? For-ever ago. Maybe never. She honestly couldn't remember being so drawn to a man.

Laughter got the better of Skye. Today had been a terrific day, and even facing her overwhelming twin wouldn't dent her happiness.

# Chapter 4

They'd both smiled a lot on the ride home. Skye had barely been able to contain herself.

From the other end of the couch, wearing only a T-shirt and panties, with a bowl of ice cream in hand, Laylee shot her another look. "You're glowing."

Skye grinned at her sister. "That's the reflection of the TV screen." Watching romantic movies with her sister was practically a tradition—one Skye generally didn't favor. Tonight though, nothing could spoil her good mood or her anticipation.

"Pretty sure it's something more." Laylee tucked her feet up beside her and then set her bowl on the end table. "When do you get the dog?"

"Nikki, the woman working at the shelter, promised we could have them in a few days. They like to check out everything first, to make sure the pets are going to good homes." She'd already explained the arrangement to Laylee, which had prompted her sister to give Ford a few longer, speculative looks.

She might not have gone into detail, at least not yet, but

when Ford had carried in two dog beds, one small for her runt, and one massive for when Maybelline visited, well, Laylee had demanded answers.

Since then, she'd been mostly quiet and introspective.

"You're serious about him."

Pretending to misunderstand, Skye asked, "Who, Ford?"

"*Who, Ford?*" Laylee repeated in a silly voice. "Don't play innocent with me. I know you too well. You actually like him."

"Well, of course I like him."

Shaking her head, Laylee clarified, "I mean, *like*-like him." To further explain, she added, "He's not like Clyde."

"Not in any way."

"Well, other than being big and gorgeous." Laylee bobbed her eyebrows. "Both men are fine eye candy."

Ford wasn't quite as big as Clyde, but what he lacked in bulk he made up for with confidence. Since neither of them were watching the movie, Skye paused it, then stood to put away their ice cream bowls.

"I'll get them," Laylee said, surprising her. "It's the least I can do after crashing in on you."

"You know I don't mind."

"Because you're always too good to me."

Her sister's mood gave Skye pause. She allowed Laylee to take the dishes, but followed her into the kitchen. Usually if her sister dropped in, it meant something was wrong. "Laylee . . ."

"I'm sorry."

Those blurted words further confused her. "For?"

While rinsing the dishes, Laylee heaved a deep sigh. After sticking the bowls and spoons in the dishwasher, she leaned back on the counter and met Skye's gaze. "For a lot of things, I guess. First, I was mean."

Taken aback, Skye pulled out a kitchen chair and sat. "When?"

Huffing a laugh, Laylee joined her at the table. "Guess I'm mean so often, you need specifics."

Skye reached across the table for her hand. "You're never mean." She was just herself, bold and fearless, charismatic and yes, a little spoiled.

"I was hitting on your neighbor." Laylee squeezed Skye's hand. "Not that he noticed, and I'm not even sure why I did it."

Skye knew why. Laylee wasn't used to being ignored, and she definitely wasn't used to a man giving more attention to Skye. None of that was important right now. "What's wrong?" When Laylee started to pull away, Skye held on. "Fess up, sis. I can tell something is bothering you."

Dramatically deflating, Laylee let her head thump onto the table. "I got dumped, and for a woman who hates me."

Drawing back in surprise, Skye stared. She hadn't known Laylee cared about a particular guy. "What do you mean, a woman who hates you?"

"She was a friend." Peeking up, Laylee said, "Or at least, I thought she was. Turns out she just wanted my guy."

"Your guy?"

Sitting up again, Laylee waved off the question. "No one important, except that he told me he was done because I wasn't a nice person. Worse, he said I'm malicious, all because I stated the truth—that my so-called friend was jealous, a user, and a man stealer."

Uh-oh. Skye scooted her chair around to sit closer to her sister. Gently, she asked, "Where were you two when you told her that?"

"At a party."

Skye winced. "So in front of people?"

Shrugging, Laylee made it clear that wasn't important. "Not like everyone didn't know when I caught the two of them making out at the party."

Worse and worse. "Making out?"

"Kissing, hugging, whatever. The party was mostly in the backyard, but she went in to get us more drinks, then he went in for something, and when he didn't return right away, *I* went in to see what was going on, and yes, there was a lot going on." Showing she was still pained by the betrayal, Laylee closed her eyes. "They were in the hall, all pressed together, and I just lost it."

"I'm sorry." Skye couldn't imagine her proud, beautiful sister suffering that kind of humiliation. "I wish you had just called me."

"Should have. It would have been better than blasting them both, because that drew attention, and pretty soon everyone knew, and then, *bam*, all of a sudden I was the bad guy."

"You and this guy were serious?"

Laylee snorted. "Not even." Her jaw clenched. "But she and I were close, or so I thought." In a rush, she asked, "Can I hang with you for a few days?"

Under these new circumstances, Skye didn't hesitate to say, "Absolutely."

Hopeful, Laylee asked, "For maybe a week or two?"

Ouch. That was tougher, but this was her sister. Differences aside, Skye loved her. "Of course."

Laylee deflated again. "You're the absolute best. All the good genes went to you."

"Ha!"

Laylee peeked at her. "Please don't do that. You are my sister, my twin, my best friend, and I think you're incredibly perfect. Just accept the compliment."

It had always been that way. Others talked about how all the best features had gone to Laylee, but Laylee insisted the opposite was true.

Dutifully, Skye whispered, "Thank you."

With that point settled, Laylee moved on. "I don't mean to be a coward, but my apartment is right next door to Marta's, and I don't want to face her until I'm ready."

"Marta is your friend?"

"Ex-friend. She burned that bridge, and I kicked the ashes. Done and done."

"Understandable." Forcing the words out, Skye said, "Stay as long as you like."

Launching from her seat, Laylee gave Skye a fierce hug. "You've always, always been the best part of me."

Hard to imagine, but Skye's amazing day had just gotten even better.

"Come on." Laylee snagged her hand and tugged her down the hall.

"Where are we going?"

"You said Ford is taking you to the restaurant tomorrow, right? And a party the week after that? We need to pick out some killer outfits for you. You're going to rock his world."

Alarmed, Skye tried to stall, but Laylee only dragged her along. "I'm not going to wear your clothes."

"I know. Ford was right. You look incredible in earth tones. You—*we*—have great skin, and the colors you choose really complement your complexion. Plus I love your hair. I mean, I love that it's different from mine, but it also totally suits you."

Er . . . "Thank you?"

Showing no compunction at all, Laylee entered Skye's bedroom and made a beeline for her closet, where she began ruthlessly rummaging through her things.

"The dinner is upscale," Skye offered. "Those dresses are in the back."

"And the party?"

"More casual, but I'll still wear a dress."

"Aha." Laylee found what she wanted. "This is going to be perfect."

\* \* \*

Seated at the restaurant table with many business friends, Skye was a bundle of nerves. She felt certain that everyone would look at her with Ford and somehow know they weren't a real couple. Worse, she kept waiting for Clyde to show up.

Leaning close to her ear so the others wouldn't hear, Ford said, "Have I told you how incredible you look?"

The way his breath teased her sent tingles down her spine. Until now, she hadn't realized that warm breath could be exciting. He'd complimented her a few times already. She assumed, at first, it had been for Laylee's benefit, and then for the benefit of her boss and coworkers.

This time, whispered so privately, felt just for her. To be sure, she looked into those mesmerizing green eyes and whispered, "Do you mean it?"

"You're by far the most striking woman I've ever known." With two fingers, he touched a tendril of hair left loose over her ear. The rest she'd twisted up and pinned for a dressier look. "Physically, I've never known a woman as perfect as you."

She started to object, but he wasn't finished.

"It's more than that though. You're stunning, for sure, but when someone meets you, they sense your compassion and caring. Speak to you for a few minutes, and your intelligence also comes through." His mouth hitched in a casual, very sexy smile. "You're the whole package, and I'm pretty sure no one is immune."

Skye had trouble breathing, much less speaking. She'd never received praise like that. Not from anyone. Her parents loved her, but they often drew unfair comparisons to Laylee. She and her sister were close, but Laylee was so energetic, always flitting around, that she seldom paused long enough to compliment. Clyde? He'd been all about her looks, and then he'd met her sister and, like most men, he'd been easily diverted. The differences between the sisters had been obvious to him, and of course, she'd come in second place. Only after Laylee laughingly turned him down did he circle back to Skye.

Ford was unlike any man she'd ever met, and her heart was quickly getting into trouble. "Thank you."

"This dress . . . It suits you in a dozen ways. The color, the simplicity." His gaze dipped over her. "On someone else, it might seem sedate. On you? It's like you set out to torture me." Three beats passed before he gave her another smile. "In the nicest possible way."

Holy smokes, he was good at this. She felt seduced, and they were sitting at a table with several people. Thankfully, the others were involved in their own conversations.

Needing something to do, Skye twisted her napkin in her hands. The body-hugging dress with an asymmetrical hemline wasn't that low-cut, and the hem landed just above her knees. She'd bought it on a whim over a year ago but hadn't had a chance to wear it. That is, not until Laylee found it in her closet.

She'd surprised Skye by choosing simple silver earrings and a delicate necklace as jewelry, much more in line with Skye's style than her own. To finish the outfit, Skye wore strappy sandals with a two-inch heel.

After all the praise she'd gotten from her sister and Ford, she truly felt beautiful.

Of course, he'd easily charmed everyone, including the Montgomery family, who'd hosted the dinner to celebrate the retirement of one of their own. Ford's manners were impeccable, his smiles engaging, and his conversation witty.

While the others chatted, he leaned close again. "Am I doing okay with the bosses?"

He was kissing close—and looking at his mouth, she was oh-so tempted. "What do you mean?"

"This dinner is important to you, I can tell. I've been on my best behavior—it helps to be successful with a sales pitch."

How could she not smile at that? "You've impressed me." Mostly just by being himself. Yes, she'd noticed a little of his slick maneuvering, but she doubted anyone else had. No wonder he was so good at his job. "And in case I didn't mention it, you look . . ." Delicious. Indescribable. Like temptation defined. "Very handsome."

Green eyes glittering, he whispered, "Your mouth said one thing, but your eyes said something else." Into her ear again, he breathed, "I'd love to know what you were really thinking."

Suddenly, from behind her, Clyde said, "She's always had expressive eyes."

Skye started, but Ford merely took her hand, unsurprised. He gave a single nod. "Clyde."

While everyone at the table greeted Clyde, Ford brushed his thumb over her knuckles. "Relax."

Easier said than done.

As Clyde turned back to them, Skye could almost swear she felt the tension arcing between the two men. Thankfully, the meal was over and even better, there were no empty seats at their table, so Clyde couldn't join them.

"Cocktails in the lounge," one of family members announced. "I hope you can all stay for a few drinks and some dancing."

Choking back a groan, she allowed Ford to tug her to her feet.

With a telling smile, he said to Clyde, "See you around," in clear dismissal.

To her, what was even more telling was that other than his initial hello, Clyde kept his distance. Oh, he watched her—often. But he didn't intrude again. Half an hour went by peacefully.

"Should I be insulted?"

The teasing words regained her attention. She and Ford were in the middle of a slow dance, and she'd been distracted. Hard to believe, with her oh-so aware of his nearness. "What?"

His hand on her back brought her marginally closer. "You left me, and here I was doing my best to behave."

His best was pretty darned good. "Behave?" He certainly didn't have to do anything special to get and hold attention. Nearly every woman in the room had checked him out multiple times. "We're only dancing."

"But there are so many ways to dance. Only I'm not Clyde, so I'm honoring your wishes."

Meaning . . . what? Tipping her head back to study him, she admitted, "I don't understand you."

"Want me to explain? I will, as long as you keep in mind that you're in charge, so no matter what I say, you don't have to worry about me overstepping, not in any way."

From the beginning, everything with him was different. The only thing that worried her was her own reaction to him. "Okay, let's hear it."

"You're nearly irresistible. A hundred times, I've thought how easy it would be to kiss you."

The flush seemed to start from her heart and expand everywhere until she was suddenly too warm.

"Like now," he said low. "With you looking like that."

Her gaze strayed to his mouth again. She could almost feel his kiss. Taste it.

Of course, his lips curved in acknowledgment. "Anything you want, Skye, just say so. You set the parameters, not me."

Bull! Staring up at him, she said, "You don't want involvement any more than I do."

"I didn't," he conceded.

That clarification rang like a bell in her brain. Breath held, she waited.

"Now?" One muscular shoulder lifted to let her know he was rethinking the situation. "I don't mind being honest . . . if you want to hear it." His attention went beyond her, and a chill replaced the heat in his eyes. "But I want no comparisons to your ape."

Maybe she should be honest, too. "I never completely trusted Clyde."

He ended the dance, right there in the middle of things. The intensity of his gaze boring into hers kept her pulse galloping. "Come on." Taking her hand, he led her off the floor and to a quieter corner. The second they stopped, he asked, "You trust me?"

It was such an enormous concession, and yet, after seeing him at the shelter, everything had changed. "I do. Is that alarming?"

"No." Muscles in his face shifted, indicating some type of struggle, until finally he said, "Thank you."

Those simple, heartfelt words got her, making an enormous difference—in everything. Stepping closer, her hands on his shoulders, she went on tiptoe . . . and kissed him.

Too soft. Too fast. Such a tease.

But kissing him had been somehow necessary.

An inferno of heat returned to his gaze, but his tone remained quiet. "There will be more of that?"

"I hope so." From the start, their relationship—first as neighbors, then as cohorts in her scheme to fend off other men—had been shallow and meaningless, the only type of relationship she'd accepted lately.

Until she'd seen Ford with her sister. Laylee hadn't beguiled him as she did so many men. Ford had joked with her, was amused by her, and seemed to understand her. But he hadn't instantly fallen under her spell.

And then with Maybelline and her tiny buddy. The love he

felt for that massive, sadly unattractive dog had been as obvious as his green eyes. She sensed patience, affection, longing, and a sort of kinship with the unwanted creature.

He clearly loved his friends, giving them not only loyalty but room to grow and love, whether their new lives included him or not.

Nothing about Ford was the norm in the men she usually encountered, so she couldn't feel the usual way about him.

"Good." He leaned back on the wall, the epitome of a man at leisure, except now she sensed an alert readiness. "Yet you keep glancing at Clyde, like you did during the dance."

Such a dolt. She'd probably offended him, and she'd never want to do that. "Sorry. It just . . . It surprises me that Clyde is keeping his distance."

"You made it clear you're not interested in him, and he can see I *am* interested in you. That's a losing combo for him, no matter how he looks at it."

*Was* he interested? With Ford, it was hard to tell. He wasn't acting overly enthusiastic about her kiss. "When it's only the two of us, you don't have to say things like that."

"I don't have to do anything." The music ended, and while people returned to their tables, they moved to the bar. "I'm enjoying myself."

"Really? This doesn't seem like your usual scene."

"Mingling for business? It's half of what I do." He ordered a cola for himself. Skye chose the same. Elbows back on the bar, he glanced around the room. "This time is different though."

"How so?"

His eyes cut to hers, easily capturing her gaze. "Because you're here."

Those words settled on her heart, *in* her heart. Did he mean them? "That's one of those things you don't have to—"

"To say. I know." Accepting the ice-filled glass handed to

him, he frowned thoughtfully, then took a sip. "It's true. You're good company."

That particular compliment had substance. It mattered, far more so than a comment on her looks. "It should be obvious that I'm enjoying your company, too."

"That tiny kiss?" he scoffed, clearly egging her on, making it sound like a challenge.

Just wait until she got him alone. Fighting a grin, she caught his hand and drew him to a more private table that was currently unoccupied. People glanced their way, but no one could hear them, so she felt safe saying, "Keep in mind that we're at a company function."

"Hmm. So once we're away from here, you'll offer more, with added intensity?"

The way he asked, she had to laugh. "Want me to spell out my intentions?"

He set his drink on the table, then took hers as well and put it aside. His warm palm settled on the side of her neck, and he stepped so close that she breathed in his scent. "I want to know what the chances are that I can be myself now, interest and all."

What a thrill to finally understand him. "I'd say one hundred percent." She rested a hand on his chest. "And I look forward to your best efforts."

Just like that, Ford changed from gracious wingman to sexy next-door neighbor, giving her the full impact of his appeal. Tone pitched low and seductive, he said, "Good to know. Holding back hasn't been easy."

So he had been? She stepped closer, too. "I promise, you don't need to. I'm not fragile."

His lips brushed her ear as he murmured, "You're red-hot temptation."

Oh, how she liked hearing that—from him.

Right beside them, Clyde said, "Well, I guess this time it is different."

The bottom dropped out of Skye's stomach. She'd momentarily forgotten where she was, and she'd most definitely forgotten about Clyde.

Ford tucked her into his side. "This shit," he said mildly, "is starting to annoy me."

To her surprise, Clyde chuckled. "Yeah, I'm sure I'd feel the same if I was you."

"You're not me."

"No, that much is clear. For the record, Skye, I'm glad."

Hearing his sincerity, she relaxed.

"Also for the record, if anything goes wrong, if he hurts you in any way, I'm still around. All you have to do is call."

She said, "I won't."

He acknowledged her words with a nod.

It surprised her again when Ford offered his hand. "Maybe I misjudged you."

"Because I acted like an ass." He accepted the friendly offering. "In your place, I'd have felt the same. I wasn't nice, and I regret it."

"Messing up had to sting."

"More than you know."

Ford glanced at her. "Believe me, I get it." He faced Clyde again. "I won't make the same mistake."

Clyde kept his attention on her. "I'd still like to be a friend."

Unwilling to let him off the hook so easily, Skye said, "I'll think about it."

"Fair enough." And just like that, Clyde walked away.

"You see," Ford said. "I know how to be useful."

That quip effectively demolished her good mood. Damn it, he could be so cryptic sometimes, and he was better at acting than she'd expected. So had any of his compliments been real?

Their last exchange, which she had seen as a turning point, a step toward a real relationship, now seemed suspect.

She turned on him so quickly that his brows shot up. Grabbing a fistful of his shirt, she asked, "Did you know Clyde had crept up on us?"

He took in her expression, then mirrored it with a frown of his own. "I'm here to look out for you, so of course I saw the putz moving in."

None of it had been real.

God, she'd been duped by her own game. Well, she still had her pride, so she gathered it around her and smiled. "*Useful* is one word for you." A glance around the room showed the thinning crowd. "With that accomplished, I think I'd like to head home."

Searching her face, Ford's frown darkened. "Fine."

Leaving was slow, with everyone taking time to say goodbye. Patience personified, Ford stayed at her side and continued to charm one and all until the two of them were in his car.

Once on the road, they both fell into an awful silence that somehow grew heavier with every mile that brought them closer to home.

Unable to take it a minute more, Skye said, "Thank you again. For everything."

He nodded. "No problem."

That should have been it, but when he pulled into her driveway instead of his own, words crowded into her head, and she knew she couldn't let it end like this. "Being a twin isn't easy."

He turned off the car, draped a forearm over the wheel and faced her. "Ups and downs, I'm sure."

"Everyone has always compared us. On everything."

"You're both gorgeous." One corner of his mouth kicked up. "Knox thought you were a supermodel."

"Laylee is. Well, she's a local model, but she still makes a ton of money."

"Guess she chooses her own hours?"

"She's selective in the jobs she takes." Awkwardness made her talk faster. "She's in high demand. She could work every day if she wanted, or only five times a year. She'd still earn enough to get by."

"You could do the same, but I'm glad you don't."

Skye shook her head. She had no interest in modeling, but it was the perfect career for her sister. "I can't tell you how many times I've heard the comparisons. People would say that they couldn't tell us apart, except my nose is thicker. My face is wider. My lips are bigger. My brows are lower." Laying it all out there made her self-conscious. "I felt like her Neanderthal cousin instead of her twin."

Ford snorted. "You're too beautiful to think that. Yes, you have strong features, but they suit you perfectly." He brushed his knuckles over her upper arm. "Are you sure those comments were made as insults?"

She honestly had no idea. "They might have been only observations, but for me they were always negative."

"You don't have a *big* nose, Skye. You have a nose that balances your incredible eyes and that sexy-as-sin mouth."

Her gaze clashed with his. "My mouth is . . . ?"

"Sexy," he repeated in that special tone that curled her toes. "So. Damned. Sexy."

Well, that was a unique compliment, especially growled in his deep voice.

"I see your mouth and think things a wingman shouldn't think." He slowly inhaled, all the while staring at her lips, making them tingle. "You have no idea what a struggle it's been."

Nice. "So these things you were thinking . . . ?"

He laughed. "Things that lead to a bed and tangled sheets, heat and sweat, and—I promise—satisfaction."

Okay, yeah, she was convinced. "It . . ." Wow, now her voice was all low and affected. She cleared her throat. "It wasn't just comments on my features that bothered me."

"So what else?"

"Laylee is always smiles and sunshine."

"You're sincerity and compassion, and that trumps a smile every time. What else?"

Her lips twitched. He was good at this, at lightening her mood and lifting her spirit. "We already covered colors."

"She's flashy, you're low-key. Different, but both good." His fingers moved down her arm until he could take her hand. "You two are different. Some people will prefer Laylee, some will prefer you. That's just how it is. Like Marcus and Bray, or Knox and me. We're all friends, but Marcus and Bray share a background. Knox and I share the same sense of humor."

"Clyde took one look at Laylee and tried his chances with her."

Scoffing, he said, "Yeah, well, we've already agreed that Clyde is an ape."

"She rejected him, and then he turned to me. I only accepted him as a friend, but he saw things most don't."

"Like the small touches of envy you and Laylee feel for each other?"

Automatic denial rushed to her tongue, but she swallowed it back. So he'd noticed that? No one else ever had, but then again, Ford was different from anyone she'd ever known. "People favor Laylee, they really do. But she thinks people take me more seriously than they do her. She thinks I get more respect."

"In some things, maybe you do. I noticed how everyone tonight wanted time with you. They're business-minded people, and they not only like you but also know you're savvy and smart, assets they appreciate and respect. Every member of the family associated with Helen's Boutiques sought you out at one point or another. From the top guns down, they wanted your input, or they just wanted to talk with you."

Realizing that he was right, her heart warmed. He did that, made her feel special in ways no one ever had. "They certainly adored you."

Discounting any praise for himself, he laughed. "You and your sister should understand that people gravitate to others because they're like-minded, or they're a good contrast. They comfort each other, or they offer challenges. People are all different, what they want and enjoy is different."

"And you? With me, I mean?" Did she still have a chance?

"Everything about you appeals to me. Your angelic face and your smoking-hot body caught me right off, but it's not just your looks. The second thing I noticed was your motivation. I mean, you're in your mid-twenties and have your own house."

"You're only a few years older than me, and you had your house before I moved in."

"It's something I always wanted."

"Me, too."

He touched her hair. "Physically, you're the hottest woman I've ever met."

To other women, that might seem shallow. To her, with the constant comparison to her twin, it was a breathtaking compliment. "You've met Laylee."

He shrugged. "She's gorgeous, too, but she's not you." A lot of meaning infused his words. "You saw Maybelline and let her slobber on you."

Grinning, she admitted, "That was a little gross, but she's a sweetheart. I wouldn't hurt her feelings."

Ford clutched his heart. "See, there's that."

"A heart attack?"

He laughed. "Oh, my God, and she's funny, too. How am I supposed to resist that?"

Going for total honesty, she said, "I wish you wouldn't resist. I wish you'd kiss me."

He paused, smiled softly, and then leaned toward her. "That would be my pleasure."

She met him halfway—and the second his mouth touched hers, that was it. In a nanosecond, they went from the "get to know you" tentative stage, to the carnal "let me devour you" phase of things. It was the kind of kiss that led to a quick stripping of clothes so naked skin could touch naked skin.

They each shifted, every small adjustment bringing them closer. His hand, so large and warm, left her neck for her shoulder, then down to her breast.

She opened several buttons of his shirt so her palm could connect with hot skin.

Then his phone buzzed, startling them both. Laboring for breath, Ford leaned back just enough to meet her gaze.

Her phone buzzed next.

"Now I'm curious," she said. "Could it be the shelter?"

That got him moving fast, lifting a hip so he could dig his phone from his pocket. He swiped the screen, then let out a breath. "Maybelline is fine. I can pick her up tomorrow."

Finally, she found her phone in her purse and checked her message. "Oh! Me, too. I mean, I get the little guy." She lowered her phone. "Ford, I need a name for him!"

"The shelter calls him Scoundrel."

She gasped. "That sweet little baby?"

It took him a second looking at her face, and then he laughed again. "Zing, right through my heart." He opened his door and came around to her side, tugged her out, and kissed her again. This time it was more of a celebratory, happy kiss. "We'll have dogs."

"The two best dogs! It's going to be so great."

Slowly, his smile slipped away. "Great, yes, but this whole thing is going to be complicated, too."

Knowing just what he meant, she agreed. "Neighbors. Maybe . . . involved?"

"I vote yes." He took her mouth, and her breath, again. "We'll be sharing our pets."

She bit her lip. "Should we wait one more day before we—"

"That's entirely up to you. I mean, I'm ready. Beyond ready. Severely ready. I was ready a week ago. But if you need more time—"

Grabbing him for another kiss was her way of answering. "Come in with me. I'll grab a change of clothes and then we can go to your house."

"Awesome plan."

Together they went up the walkway to the door. It opened before Skye could even touch the knob.

Laylee stood there, hands on hips, her fair hair in a high ponytail, looking amazing as always. With a cheek-splitting grin on her face, she drawled, "*Finally.* I was starting to think we were back in high school, making out in the driveway before Dad made us come in."

"That was *you*," Skye said, drawing Ford in with her as Laylee stepped back. "I never made out in the driveway."

"Fibber! You literally just did. Sucking face, pawing each other—such a show you put on for the neighbors."

Ford laughed at Laylee. "You were the only one gawking."

And still, all his smiles and teasing were for her. Practically floating with happiness, Skye said, "You two chat while I grab a few things."

Laylee made a big show of surprise. "You floozy!" In a loud, mockingly scandalized stage whisper, she asked Ford, "Is she spending the night with you?"

On her way down the hall, she heard Ford say, "God, I hope so. Driveways might be good enough for you, but when it comes to your sister, I need a lot more space—and a lot more time."

As her sister's hilarity filled the air, peace settled around Skye.

A night with her hot neighbor.

A night with Ford.

She could barely wait.

# Chapter 5

Staring at the ceiling, his chest still rising and falling as Skye lay soft and warm against him, Ford knew that he'd just had the best sex of his life. Nothing else would compare. No other woman, no other experience.

He'd hit a peak, and unless he could seal the deal with her, it'd all be downhill from this.

He tucked in his chin to see her face, and yeah, that was a happy smile curving her delectable mouth. Unable to resist, he pressed a kiss to her forehead. "You just ruined me."

Warm breath teased his damp skin with her throaty laugh. "Ruined you how?"

"For anyone else."

Going still, and then scowling, she jerked up to show him her displeasure. "Seriously, Ford? You're already thinking of other women?"

She was so pretty with her flushed skin and mussed hair that her disgruntlement entertained him. "Yeah." He brushed back her hair. "How other women have lost all appeal."

"Oh." The frown lifted and another smile crept in. "In that case, you're forgiven."

Curious, he asked, "What were you thinking?"

"That it was the best decision I ever made when I interrupted your party."

"It wasn't a party," he denied. "But we do get together often. You'll be okay with that?"

"Depends on whether I'm invited to take part."

Funny how life could change so quickly. "You're invited, always, from now until the end of time."

Yeah, that sounded serious enough to get her attention. Thoughtfully, she dragged the sheet around herself and sat up.

He immediately tugged it away. "I sense a heavy discussion about to happen, and I'd prefer to take part without this stellar view hidden."

Her chin hitched up. "If you expect me to be shy, you'll be disappointed."

For an answer, he wadded up the sheet and tossed it off the bed. Scooting up to sit against the headboard, he crossed his ankles and said, "Go."

After a startled laugh, she mimicked his pose. "I'm not the type to date multiple partners. If I'm seeing you, it'll only be you."

"Totally works for me." Especially since, as he'd said, there was no one who would compare to her. Before this, he hadn't known how territorial he could be. He wanted only her, and he wanted her to feel the same about him. "Consider us monogamous. That's a big step for me, so if you want to show some appreciation, I wouldn't mind."

"Thank you. It's a big step for me as well."

True, but for far different reasons. He'd dated extensively; she'd hardly dated at all. Sounding as solemn as she had, he repeated her words. "Thank you."

She chewed her bottom lip, her expression troubled. "Since we'll be sharing responsibility for the dogs, I think if you're going to be out late, I'd like to know why."

"Work only keeps me late for parties with clients, and since they always include a plus-one, I'd love for you to go with me whenever you can. Otherwise, now that I'll be a dog owner"— and he'd have Skye Fairchild waiting—"I'll plan to be home no later than six. How about you?"

"I'm usually home by four. I can tend to the dogs then. On the days when I might be later, I'll let you know."

"Good." So far, he loved her plans. "Anything else?"

Another bite of her plump lip, then she asked, "Will you tell me about your childhood, about growing up as an only kid, how and when you decided to move here, stuff like that?"

Before he thought better of it, he groaned. He hated talking about his past. Overall, his method of dealing with it had been to pretend it never existed.

Her small, cool hand touched his shoulder. "Hey, no biggie. I shouldn't have pried."

He covered her hand with his own. "No, I shouldn't have been a dramatic ass. It's not a secret, just something I try to ignore. If you won't be too bored, I'll give you the broad strokes."

"Nothing about you could ever bore me."

The way she said that inspired hope that she, too, was invested. "Is that so?"

"You've fascinated me since the first day I moved here and saw you cutting grass. I'd never seen anyone look so good getting sweaty."

His childhood was a bramble of disappointments and determination, yet still he smiled. "You like the hot and overworked look, is that it?"

"On you, I like every look." She peered over his body, from his shoulders to his abdomen, down to his toes and up his legs, then lingered. "This look, in a bed and naked, is my favorite so far."

"You're welcome to the view whenever you want."

Her lips lifted into a grin. "So at any moment, I could command you to strip?"

"As long as you strip with me."

They grinned together, until she traced his mouth. "Ford, is this your way of avoiding those broad strokes?"

Another groan tried to break free, but he swallowed it back. "Of course not." *Liar.* "I don't know where to begin."

"Tell me why you decided to leave your home," she said, encouraging him.

"It was never a home. Just a house that fell apart a little more each year." His own house was well maintained, and it looked as nice as he could make it, but in many ways, it didn't yet feel like a home, either. "For as long as I can remember, Mom and Dad were both nasty drunks." That was broad enough that she could probably guess the rest, but he filled in some details anyway. "From weekend binges to midweek meltdowns and missed work. Good employment turned to temp work. I'm not sure why they stayed married, because they spent more time fighting than anything else."

Putting her head on his shoulder, Skye whispered, "That sounds awful."

It was, in more ways than she could realize. "We were the joke of the neighborhood. It was nothing to see cop cars at our house because Mom would call on Dad, or vice versa, whenever they really got piss-faced, and that happened often enough. I was probably around ten or so when I decided I'd be different." Young and proud, but unsure how to navigate the ridicule he'd faced on a daily basis.

"I can't even imagine how hard that had to be for a kid."

"At the time, yeah, I hated my life, and I hated them. Looking back, I think that's where I learned the gift of gab. At least, it's served me well as a pharmaceutical rep."

"I don't understand."

"Kids love to poke fun. Not to be cruel or to bully, not always anyway. Show me a teenager and I'll show you a moody kid trying to figure out his life. Everyone has their own stuff to deal with. Joking about yourself and your friends helps. So my group would often point out the drunken antics of my folks." He considered the past for a quiet moment. "It was humiliating, but it also taught me how to deal with stuff. They'd poke fun and I'd join in. Like, someone would say how my dad was in the road in his boxers, stumbling around. I'd tell them it was even worse when he was drunk—because everyone already knew he was hammered."

A smile, small and sad, touched her mouth. "You turned the joke in your favor."

"It had people laughing with me instead of at me."

"I doubt they ever laughed at you."

Putting his head back, he closed his eyes. "In fifth grade, I failed a test, so the teacher called my mom for a conference." Shame burned him again, making the words catch in his throat. "She showed up at the school completely tanked. Threatened the teacher and the principal. Cops were called—nothing new for the Caruso family—and Mom spent the day in the local jail." He huffed a short laugh devoid of humor. "Dad was pissed beyond reason. He trashed the house and threatened to . . ." No, he wouldn't share the idiotic threats of the man who'd fathered him. Rubbing his face, he let that memory go and lightened the mood. "Anyway, it taught me what I didn't want to be, you know?"

She nodded, her expression a little devastated.

Ford hauled her close so that she rested against his chest. Against his heart. "Growing up wasn't fun, but it toughened me up, and I learned to navigate. I never failed another test, that's for sure. Straight As for me. Soon as I had enough credits to graduate, I got my diploma, grabbed what I could from home, and took off."

"How old were you?"

"Seventeen. Old enough." At least it had felt that way at the time. "I had money saved from various jobs, my own used car, and a lot of unrealistic plans."

"What did you do? How did you survive?"

At first, it hadn't been easy. "I got a night job cleaning the floors at a grocery, and that led to meeting the pharmacist there. Great guy who taught me to golf, and during those lessons he imparted a lot of terrific advice. With him guiding me, I got my associate's degree, then my bachelor's, and that led to a job as a pharmaceutical rep. In a lot of ways, I was made for this job."

"Have you ever been back home?"

"For what? It was a roof over my head, but never a home."

"Your dad . . ."

"Not anyone's idea of a father figure. When I try hard enough, I can remember a handful of good times with my mom, all of them when I was really young, and all short-lived. She didn't physically abuse me or anything. Mostly, she just ignored my existence, and when she couldn't do that, she resented me. Sometimes she relied on me." The truth still hurt. "But she never loved me."

Skye hugged him so fiercely, she stole his breath. "I pity them. They missed out on an awesome son."

There was her big heart again, knowing the right thing to say. "Not sure what they'd think of me now, and I don't care enough to find out. Going back isn't an option, and most of the time I forget all about them." *Most of the time.* "I'll tell you one thing. If I'm ever a dad, I'll be totally different. My parents taught me what not to be, what not to do, and they showed me how I didn't want to live my life. Lessons well learned." Lessons he'd never forget. "They wasted so much time and energy on the wrong things."

"Drinking and fighting."

"Yes." He teased his fingertips over her downy cheek, her chin, then tipped up her face so he could look into her midnight eyes, ensuring she understood his conviction. "I won't make those mistakes. No child of mine will ever have to wonder if I'll have a job to support them or to be sure they have what they need. They won't have to wonder whether I'll be sober and reasonable, or whether I'll take care of them."

"If you'll love them."

He vowed, "I'll love him or her so much, they'll never have doubts."

The way she looked at him, with so much faith, warmed him even before she spoke. "Any child would be lucky to have you as a father."

The words finished him off. Where had she been all his life? How had he not known that someone like her existed, or that she'd be so vital to him?

What she said mattered a lot, and he needed time to take it in. "Let's talk about your childhood."

Though he could tell she wasn't fooled by his switch of topic, she humored him. "Compared to your upbringing, mine was easy. The hardest thing I had to deal with were comparisons to Laylee. Did I tell you my father was a twin? You'd think he would have understood, but he was the"—she made air quotes—"*smart twin.* That's how my grandparents characterize him. My dad was the smart twin and my uncle was the athletic twin." She rolled her eyes. "Neither Laylee nor I is athletic. For us it's the smart, serious twin"—she aimed a thumb at her chest—"and the beautiful, fun-loving twin, meaning Laylee."

He cupped a hand to her cheek. "It's a fact of life that even good parents aren't perfect. The most important things are whether you felt loved and cared for."

"I did, absolutely. Not just by my parents, but we're close

to our grandparents on both sides, and we have a bunch of aunts, uncles, and cousins that we see often." Trying to look cavalier, she asked, "Will I get to introduce you to all of them?"

Another promising sign, that she'd even want him to meet her family. He didn't think Skye would do that unless she wanted him to be a fixture in her life. "I'd be happy to meet them." If he could win them over, it'd give him an edge.

She blinked, grinned, and ended up laughing. "You are the most amazing man. My family is going to love you."

"That's funny?"

"The quintessential bachelor happy to meet my large family? It's a little funny, but I should have known you'd be fine with it. You're the most adaptive person I've ever met. Nothing makes you uneasy."

He snorted at that. Everything made him uneasy, most especially the idea of screwing up with her. "You aren't worried that I'll schmooze your family?"

"You're more genuine than you think. Do you not realize how open and friendly you are? People are drawn to you. They like you immediately. You say two or three things, and they feel like they've known you forever. You're automatically a friend." She leaned in to kiss the corner of his mouth. "It's a gift." Yawning, she settled against him again, curving her body as close to his as she could get. "I like us together, making plans."

Yeah, he liked that a lot.

He especially liked that she saw in him things he'd never seen in himself. Wonderful things that made him optimistic even though he hadn't been feeling exactly pessimistic. More like . . . detached. Almost separate from others.

Sometimes lonely.

But now, after sharing details of his life that he'd never shared with anyone else, everything was good, perfect even.

He reached over the side of the bed for the sheet and settled it on them, then pulled up the quilt so she wouldn't be chilled in the air-conditioning.

Tomorrow they'd bring home the dogs. He'd have Maybelline, he'd have Skye. The future looked so bright.

With one last hug, he kissed her bare shoulder, enjoying the faint way she murmured to him, then closed his eyes in extreme contentment.

This was meant to be.

Skye flopped down onto the couch, utterly exhausted. She'd been so excited about adopting the dogs, but after only two days, she knew she needed to reevaluate.

"How was your party?" Laylee asked, settling beside her and handing her a bottle of water.

Wearily, Skye turned her head to face her sister. "The party was fine, but the dogs trashed Ford's house."

"Ugh. How bad?" Without giving Skye a chance to answer, she said, "It was the monstrous dog, right? She probably ate everything in sight and broke everything she sat on."

Skye locked her teeth until she could speak reasonably. "Actually, no. Maybelline is a gentle sweetheart, and the worst damage she did was to dig around on Ford's bed, rearranging all his bedding to create a nest."

Laylee choked. "I specifically remember you two buying a massive bed for her."

"I think she wanted Ford's scent. When he leaves for work tomorrow, he's going to try leaving a T-shirt in her bed to see if that helps."

"Well, he does smell nice."

"Right?" Skye agreed. Ford was absolutely delicious. Secretly, she wanted one of his shirts to sleep with, too. "It seems my little rascal did most of the damage." She wrinkled her nose. "He peed. On everything."

"OMG."

"Ford said he was marking his territory. If so, he owns the whole house now."

Laylee burst out laughing.

"Luckily, he couldn't get on the bed, the rascal." Aggrieved, she gave a long sigh. "When I tried to bring him home with me, you'd have thought I was taking Maybelline's heart, the way the two of them carried on. Ford suggested they just stay the night with him." Which made her feel as if she'd abandoned him to deal with everything.

"So let's see." Laylee eyed her critically. "Knowing my sis like I do, I bet you helped to clean up everything before you left?"

"Of course, I did. My dog made the messes. Believe me, we'd be able to tell the difference between him piddling and Maybelline." Groaning, she put her head back on the couch. It was after midnight, and she'd hoped to have some private time with Ford, but there was no way either of them would have closed the dogs out of the bedroom, not after they'd just spent all that time alone, and sleeping with both dogs basically meant not sleeping.

So Ford had kissed her, then insisted she go home to get some rest. Tomorrow was another day.

"I think we can still make this work," Skye said, trying to infuse some optimism into the words. "It's just that the dogs don't do very well being alone for so long."

Laylee raised her hand. "So maybe I can offer a solution."

Barely keeping her eyes open, Skye said, "Let's hear it."

"I'll be your dog sitter."

Skye got one eye open. "Come again?"

"Your pup is adorable, and he loves me."

"I can't take him from Maybelline." The little scoundrel might tolerate it, with Laylee to love him, but Maybelline would be miserable. Never would she do that.

With less enthusiasm and conviction, Laylee promised, "I'll watch Maybelline, too."

That got both of Skye's eyes open. "You're scared of Maybelline."

"A little, but I'm sure I'll get used to her."

Sitting straighter now, Skye scrutinized her sister. "Why?"

"I'm not ready to return to my apartment yet. If I'm going to freeload here, I can at least try to be useful."

Chewing that over, Skye decided it might be a good solution. "It would only be while we're away at work."

"And when you get home at four, you can take over again. See? Problem solved."

Grabbing her phone, Skye texted Ford the plan.

He liked it—or at least he was willing to give it a try, and that was good enough for now.

She turned to her sister with a smile. "Ford agreed, and I'm okay with it."

"Yay." Laylee hugged her. "I have a purpose. Now I can stop eating all your ice cream." While Skye laughed, Laylee stood and then pulled her to her feet. "You're slap-happy. Time for you to get some sleep."

Sleeping with Ford again would be better, but honestly, she was so tired, she was more than ready to crash.

One way or another, this would all work out. The dogs just needed a little more time to settle in, and with Laylee's help, they shouldn't have a repeat of today's total destruction.

One week later, Ford was ready to pull out his hair.

He'd envisioned plenty of private time with Skye, not necessarily in the bedroom—though he sure wasn't opposed to that—but sitting together on the couch, the dogs cuddling with them. Or long walks talking while the animals got fresh air. Playing fetch in his backyard. Swimming in his pool, with Maybelline and Tank lounging on the deck in the sunshine.

Ha!

Everything that could go wrong, had. The dogs, who'd been oh-so angelic at the shelter, had a terrible time adjusting to being "home." He still loved them, and he didn't regret having them. God, no. He looked at Maybelline and no matter what, his heart felt full. Even Skye's dog, that little rascal, still amused him.

But the destruction. It occupied most of their time. Cleaning up dog poo with Skye somehow wasn't as appealing as the scenarios he'd had in mind.

He had hoped that Laylee's offer to puppy sit would solve the problem.

But no, it most definitely had not.

Ford had to give Laylee credit for trying, yet every single day there was a new catastrophe. Today he'd deliberately arrived home before Skye, only to find Laylee on her knees scrubbing a corner of the kitchen while casting worried looks at the dogs.

Poor Skye. She'd arrived home shortly after, and it took only a single look to know she wasn't getting enough sleep.

He'd offered to clean up, but both women had suggested he take the dogs back to his house while they got things in order. Not how he'd wanted to spend the evening, but he'd reluctantly agreed.

Later, they'd eaten dinner on his back porch and of course, that was fine. As long as he and Skye were around, the dogs behaved. Unfortunately, they both had to work.

Over the next few days, Skye settled on a name for her dog: Tank. As in a water tank, since he sprinkled often. Ford thought the name worked because the runt considered himself as invincible as a tank.

She took a day off work to help get the dogs settled, and reported that they were angels.

The next day, with Skye back at work, Ford made a point of

taking off early. He got home, parked, and jogged to Skye's house, hoping Laylee would have a good report.

Instead, he found her sitting on the couch near tears, beautifully rumpled. Her hair, currently in a high, messy bun, listed to one side. She wore no makeup, and her usually stylish clothes had been replaced with well-worn yoga pants and an oversized Aerosmith T-shirt.

All around her, the house was a wreck. Tank chewed on a flip-flop, and Maybelline was sprawled out a good distance away, her head on her front paws, her expression glum. That was, until she saw him.

Ford took it all in with one sweeping glance and decided Maybelline was the top priority. Kneeling down, he opened his arms and the dog shot forward with undiluted glee.

Laughing, he sat against the wall so she couldn't knock him over. She snuffled his face and neck, howled with happiness, and finally, after wearing herself out, flopped onto her back with her head in his lap, staring up at him adoringly.

Ford rearranged himself to better accommodate her, accepting the fact that Laylee, clearly, wasn't cut out for puppy sitting. Thank God he'd gotten home early, or Maybelline would still be miserable. He couldn't bear it.

Tank, also excited, yapped around him, the footwear forgotten. He scooped up the rascal and settled him next to Maybelline's neck. "You guys missed me, huh?"

Happy barking and wiggling gave him all the answer he needed.

"I'm sorry," Laylee said. "I know I suck, but your dog hates me."

Oh, no. He wouldn't let her put the blame on Maybelline. "She doesn't hate anyone." He kissed her furry head to reassure her.

"You saw how she was looking at me."

Yes, and he'd seen where Laylee was sitting—well apart

from the dogs. Was that what Maybelline had to put up with every day? "Who made all the mess?" He was guessing Tank.

"Tank is so sweet part of the time, but the rest of the time he's a Tasmanian devil on a rampage."

Ford could guess the problem. Laylee couldn't exclusively pay attention to Tank, because that always drew Maybelline closer. Left to his own devices, Tank got into mischief. Now Ford had to decide what to do about it. They couldn't continue like this. The dogs, and Laylee, were miserable.

She heaved a sigh. "Maybelline dumped in the kitchen again."

Already knowing the answer, he asked, "Did you take her for a walk?"

She eyed him as if he was nuts. "Sorry, but I'm not attempting to walk that beast."

Maybelline gave her patented low grumble, as if insulted.

"Oh my God, you see?" Yanking her feet up onto the couch as if to protect them, she pointed at the dog. "That's what she does. She growls at me."

He was deciding how to answer when Skye walked in. She glanced around, much as he had, then pinned a smile on her face. "Hey, everyone." The dogs abandoned Ford and raced to Skye.

Gratified, he watched her react much as he had. She tossed aside her purse with a laugh and knelt down. Maybelline did knock her over, but Skye loved it. From her back, she hugged Maybelline while Tank licked her face.

Laylee, he noticed, looked wretched, and as she spoke, she sounded heartbroken, too. "Why do they love you guys so much, but hate me?"

Ford got to his feet. "You just need to give them a chance." He leaned over Skye and managed to sneak a kiss between Tank and Maybelline's snuffles.

"The big one growls at me all the time."

Skye laughed. "She's not growling, silly. She's murmuring, probably in protest at your attitude." Skye sat up, and Maybelline immediately settled beside her, luxuriating in the strokes and hugs she received. "She won't bite, you know. She's the gentlest dog ever."

Unconvinced, Laylee crept over to stand behind Ford, using him as a shield.

Maybelline looked at her and murmured.

"She's still growling!"

Ford tried, unsuccessfully, to get Laylee out from behind his back. "That's not growling. Look." He stepped away and put his hand in front of Maybelline. She nudged it for a pet. "She just wants attention."

"She would bite me."

Barely resisting the urge to roll his eyes, Ford decided to prove his point. "Never." He put his hand *in* Maybelline's mouth—and the worst he got was slobber. "Come here. Let me show you."

She rapidly backed up. "No way."

Going for a different approach, Ford straightened and looked her in the eyes. "I'll tell everyone your sister is braver than you."

Laylee snorted. "Get real. Everyone already knows that. Nothing shakes Skye."

Okay, obviously that tactic wouldn't work. It didn't help that Maybelline continued to stare at Laylee. He saw it as a longing to be her friend. Laylee, however, couldn't seem to get past her fear.

Tank walked over to her, and Laylee picked him up. "At least this one doesn't growl at me."

"Look at Maybelline's eyes," he encouraged. Her eyes were soulful, full of worry and hope, and a desperate need to be loved. She saw how Laylee held the littler dog and badly wanted to take part.

Inhaling a shaky breath, Laylee glanced at Maybelline— then away, her discomfort palpable.

Ford's heart broke a little. How many people had reacted that same way to poor Maybelline? She couldn't help her appearance, and to him it didn't matter.

To him, she was beautiful.

Seeing his disappointment, tears welled in Laylee's eyes. "I'm sorry."

Skye nodded her understanding. "It's okay, Laylee. I'll figure out something else. You don't need to watch Maybelline anymore."

Those words, letting her off the hook, only seemed to upset Laylee more. Ford could tell she wanted to be there for her sister. But as she'd said, she wasn't as strong or courageous as Skye. Not as compassionate or intuitive either.

"I have dinner ready, if you're hungry."

That was Laylee's way of trying to make up for the things she couldn't do. Ford said, "In a bit." For now, he just wanted to give the dogs the attention they needed.

"Okay, well, I'll get you both a drink, then." Fleeing into the kitchen, maybe to cry a little, Laylee disappeared with Tank.

Ford sat on the chair behind Skye. In a low whisper so Laylee wouldn't hear, he said, "You see. Massive differences between you two." He brushed his nose against her hair, breathing in her scent and grateful to have her in his life, sharing his love of their dogs. "I saw those differences right off."

Tipping her head back, she accepted the soft, upside down kiss he gave her. With her hand to his jaw, she promised, "We *will* figure this out. We're in this together—for both dogs. They'll get the love and attention they deserve."

Every day, in a new and different way, Skye showed him how special she was. He was still smiling at her when a brisk knock sounded on the door. Maybelline lifted her big head, alert but not alarmed.

Laylee, a little red eyed, stepped back into the room. "Who—"

She didn't get out another word before Tank launched himself from her arms. Skye gasped, Ford made a wild grab but missed, and Tank hit the floor like a furry cannonball. He rolled, shot back to his feet, and prepared to demolish whoever came through the door.

Hand to her heart, Laylee said, "*Ohmigod*, I'm so sorry!"

Of course, Skye rallied. "It's okay," she said a little too fast, still shaken. "He's okay. I'm okay. We're all okay."

Maybelline got up and snuffled close to Tank. Oddly enough, that calmed the little dog, at least enough that Ford could take a breath.

Bedlam, he decided. It was all bedlam instead of the paradise he'd imagined. But looking at Skye, composed instead of overwhelmed, and her sis, devastated at her perceived shortcomings, and the two dogs, so strongly bonded, he knew he'd rather be in bedlam here, with Skye and her sister and the two best dogs in the world, than back in his peaceful single lifestyle.

He managed a smile. "Skye, can you restrain Tank?" She leaned forward enough to catch the rascal and cradle him protectively in her arms. "Laylee, calm down. No harm done." Laylee drew in a slow breath, but it was a shuddery sound, still very close to a sob. "Maybelline, good girl." He gave her ear a gentle rub and, with everyone as calm as he could manage in the moment, opened the door.

Knox stood there with Paul, a guy Ford had met several times. "Hey, what's up?"

Knox didn't reply. He stared beyond Ford into the house, and when Ford turned, he saw nearly the same expression on Laylee's face. Huh. Their connection was so electric, static danced in the air.

Paul grinned. "He's gone into a stupor."

"Seems so." Ford opened the door wider. "Come on in, Paul, before the dogs get out. See if you can drag Knox along."

Suddenly Laylee gasped, put a hand to her falling hair, and went bright red. "You didn't say we'd have company!"

"It's not company," Ford reasoned. "It's just Knox and Paul."

"That's the definition of company!" Pivoting sharply, she went down the hall at a fast clip. In a more moderate tone, she said, "I'll be right back."

Skye snickered. "Well, that was interesting." Still with Tank held close, she offered her hand. "Hi. I'm Skye Fairchild."

Paul did a double take. "Twins?"

"Yes. I think we took my sister, Laylee, by surprise."

Knox continued staring at where Laylee had disappeared. "I didn't know you had a sister."

Ford noticed that he didn't say *twin*. He'd bet money that Knox, like him, saw the uniqueness of each woman. "As you can see by the destruction, we've had our hands full with the dogs."

Leaning close, Skye whispered, "They're giving my sister fits."

Knox got himself together. "I just finished a big roofing job, so I finally have a little time to measure your yard for a fence. Maybe that'll help. Paul's going to lend a hand. He was in construction with me until he bailed to be a dog walker."

Ford jerked around and met Skye's alert gaze. Together they asked, "Dog walker?" with a lot of hope.

"Much more fun than sweating balls on a roof." Paul gave Tank a couple of friendly scratches, then moved on to Maybelline. "And who is this beautiful girl?"

Maybelline put her face up for some love, and Paul, bless him, bent to deliver, even kissing her on her knobby head. "Yes, you're a sweetheart, aren't you? Look at those expressive eyes. Yes, baby. Such a good dog." When Maybelline delivered a wet lick to Paul's head, he only laughed and used a shoulder to swipe his face. "When Knox said you got a dog, I didn't expect a dog like this. She's adorable."

*Adorable.* Seeing a solution to their problem, Ford grabbed Paul into a giant bear hug.

"What the hell?" Knox said. "I didn't even get a hello."

"You," Ford replied, while still smothering Paul, "were busy drooling after Laylee."

Paul finally freed himself. "I'm getting all this love . . . why?"

"You're just what I need."

Knox, still keeping an eye on the hall where Laylee had fled, chimed in. "Sorry, Ford, you missed your chance. Paul is now in a committed relationship."

"Not that you aren't a great guy." Giving Ford a thwack on the shoulder, Paul grinned. "A little pretty for my tastes, but still." He confided to Skye, "Joking aside though, Ford is a solid guy despite his devastating handsomeness."

"He is gorgeous, isn't he?"

Paul sighed. "Yes, but he's also a hard worker with a great job, and he's funny even when he doesn't mean to be." He winked at Skye. "Best of all, whenever I've needed something, he's there."

"Same," Knox said. "I like to give him crap, but he's a catch."

Ford sputtered. The compliments from Paul didn't bother him, but from Knox, he kept waiting for a punchline.

When none came, he put his arm over Paul's shoulders. "He knows men far better than Knox, so you can take his word for it."

"I already know all about Ford's great qualities." Expression soft and full of emotion, Skye said, "That's why I'm already half in love with him."

Taken by surprise, Ford opened his mouth but no words emerged. She wasn't the first woman to say such a thing to him, but she was the first who really mattered to him, and this was the first time he wanted it to be true.

And she'd made that statement with two of his friends

standing there, rather than in a private moment. Deliberate timing on her part? Was she nervous about his reaction?

Paul nudged him hard. "Now is when you speak."

He sucked in an audible breath, then shouted, "*Laylee.*"

She yelled back, "What?"

Without taking his gaze from Skye, he announced, "Your sister and I are going to my house for five minutes. You have to come out and play hostess."

She screeched, which had Knox grinning.

To Paul, he said, "Don't go anywhere. Seriously. We need to talk."

"I'll just entertain the dogs until you return." He took Tank from Skye and shooed the two of them away.

Grabbing Skye's hand, Ford hurried her out the kitchen door to the backyard, then over to his patio. She hadn't yet said she loved him, only that she was halfway there. He'd do his utmost to tip her over the line.

"Ford," she laughingly complained, practically running to keep up.

Under the awning, away from prying eyes, he turned her, pressed her to the door, and took her mouth in a kiss meant to convey everything he felt, including things he had no experience articulating.

"Mmm," she murmured, and as soon as he let up, she said, "I know none of this was in your plan."

"It was your plan. But let's forget it." He kissed her again. Left uninterrupted, he could have gone on kissing her all day. All week.

A lifetime would suit him.

She gently pressed him away. "Does this mean you don't mind?"

"That you're falling for me? No, I don't mind because I'm doing the same."

"Loving yourself?" Far too seriously, she said, "You should, you know. Everything Paul said is true. For a hundred different reasons, you're an incredible person."

Bemused, he shook his head. "I meant that I feel the same about you. I like how things are going—added emotion and all."

"You're sure?"

How could she not know how special she was? "It's my fault that you aren't already certain. I was trying not to rush you, but if you recall, you were upfront about not wanting anything to do with a romantic relationship."

Her grin went crooked. "Sounds like it's my fault, not yours. And you're right. I was adamant—until I saw you with Maybelline. Or maybe it was before that, when you were amused by Laylee instead of panting after her."

Laylee was sweet, but she wasn't for him. "Knox is panting, FYI."

"I noticed. I hope Laylee gives him a chance."

Watching her closely to gauge her reaction, he said, "I love how you are with Maybelline. How you are with everyone, including me."

She ducked her face, but only for a moment. Then she stepped against him and squeezed him tight. "This little chat has been enlightening."

"Hasn't it?" He was rather pleased with how things were going, too. He wanted to talk to her more, to explain . . . everything. How much he cared. That he was in it for the long haul. He wanted to promise her so many things, but they had people waiting for them. "Should we get back over there before your sister scares off Knox and Paul?"

"Yes." With new excitement, she said, "We need to convince Paul to be our dog walker. That would be a huge help, right?"

"He's exactly what we need." With Paul's assistance, maybe Ford would finally have everything, including time enough to prove to Skye how good they were together.

Taking his hand, Skye started them back across the lawns. "The fence will be great, too." She peeked up at him. "Maybe if Laylee can just let the dogs into the yard, they'll be less destructive."

"We can hope."

They both laughed, and that was the best thing about Skye. She was undoubtedly tired, her house was a mess, but she still embraced life, and the dogs. . . .

And him.

They'd made a lot of progress today. Soon, they'd have it all worked out.

# Chapter 6

Skye was hustling to get out the door on time. Hiring Paul as a daily dog walker had made a world of difference. In the past two weeks, the fence had almost been completed, and their lives had calmed down considerably. The dogs still made occasional messes in their houses, and she didn't yet have all the time she wanted with Ford, but she was optimistic.

On the one hand, she'd never been happier. Ford had so effortlessly stolen her heart that she didn't even miss it. On the other hand, they were trying to keep up two households with two mismatched pets, work their busy jobs, and pursue a hot new romance all at the same time. There were days when she saw Ford a lot, and days when they seemed to spend all their time corralling animals and cleaning.

As she stepped to the right of her hallway to hurriedly move around Laylee, her sister had the same idea, and they nearly collided.

Skye flattened to the wall to make room, but to her surprise, Laylee just stood there . . . her face crumpling.

Oh, no. "Laylee?"

Sniffling, her sister blinked fast, muttered, "Sorry," and started to dart away.

"Wait."

Lifting a hand, Laylee sailed past. "You're in a hurry. I didn't mean to get in your way."

Watching her duck into the spare bedroom—a room she now considered Laylee's—Skye came to a decision. She had ten minutes before she needed to go to work. She had planned to grab a bite to eat, but that could wait. Laylee needed her.

Moving to the closed bedroom door, she knocked softly, turned the knob, and stepped in. Laylee sat on the side of the bed, her posture dejected.

"Sorry." Swiping at her face, likely removing tears, Laylee said, "I'm fine, I swear. I know you're in a rush, and I promise nothing is wrong." She forced a grin that looked somewhat sickly. "It's just me being me. You know what I mean."

"No, I don't." Never before had Laylee held back. Usually, she bombarded Skye with everything she felt, did, or wanted. Of course, Skye had been so busy in the last couple of weeks, she and Laylee had barely talked lately.

That wasn't fair to her sister.

Sitting beside Laylee, Skye took her hand. It was still damp with tears, and that made Skye a little teary-eyed, too.

Suddenly, Laylee turned and hugged her. Voice choked, she whispered, "I really, really am sorry. You've got enough on your plate without me adding to it."

"You're my sister." For Skye, it was as simple as that. "If you hurt, I hurt."

Issuing a watery laugh, Laylee released her and reached for a clean tissue on the nightstand. "I don't want that." She mopped at her face, then sighed. "I'm such a wuss. About everything."

"Not true, but if you want to tell me the particular thing that has you upset right now, I might be able to help."

"I canceled the lease on my apartment."

Unprepared for that bombshell, Skye asked, "When did that happen?"

"Yesterday, I drove over to my place to get a few more things. My big, bold plan was to ignore Marta if I saw her. I swear, Skye, I felt all righteous and ready to face her down."

Skye stroked Laylee's hair. "But?"

"He was there with her."

Wincing for her sister, Skye asked, "Your ex?"

She nodded. "Just as I was going into my apartment, they were coming out of Marta's. Laughing, kissing." Laylee fell back on the bed, her forearm over her eyes. "They were happy."

Stretching out beside her, Skye stared at the ceiling. "That had to be awful." She imagined how she'd feel if that happened with Ford, and she knew she'd be in the same shape. "I'm sorry."

Lowering her arm, Laylee turned to face Skye. "I had hoped I'd be a help to you, but I haven't been."

"That's not true." Skye also rolled to her side, propping herself up on her elbow and using the other hand to lace her fingers with Laylee's. "You often have food ready when Ford and I get home. You've done the grocery shopping for me."

"But I've been useless where the dogs are concerned."

Love for her sister made her a smile. "True, you haven't warmed up to Maybelline. But with Paul now walking the dogs in the middle of the day, there haven't been nearly as many issues. In a few more days the yards will be fenced, and then all you'll need to do is let them out."

Laylee shook her head. "You don't need me. You're the

most self-sufficient person I know. Until Ford, you didn't even care about having a date. Now, with him, the last thing you need is a sister hanging around all the time."

Skye sat up so Laylee would get the full force of her sternest frown. "You are my sister and I love you. I will *always* need you. Always, Laylee."

Swallowing heavily, Laylee sat up, too. "I'm in your way."

"Don't say things like that because it pisses me off."

Her mouth screwed to the side. "Ford is influencing your language."

"Ford is amazing. I'm in love with him."

"That's what I'm saying." Half laughing, half crying, Laylee smiled at her. "He loves you, too."

Forgetting her rush, Skye grabbed those words and held them tight. "Do you really think so?"

"Good grief." Laylee gave her an affectionate push. "You can't tell? Because anyone can see it."

"You're sure?"

"Skye." This time Laylee smoothed Skye's hair. "For real, you're the best sister in the entire world. The most amazing, most generous, sweetest person I know. But you've never been that great at understanding guys."

"They're complicated."

"Nah. *We're* complicated." Laylee grinned. "Thankfully, guys are awesomely basic. Most of the time anyway." She gave that quick thought and added, "Good guys, I mean. Creeps are everywhere, but Ford is definitely not a creep, and he most definitely *is* in love with you."

Skye agreed that he wasn't a creep. He was the most protective, bighearted, insightful, and caring man she'd ever known. "So what do I do?"

"Tell Ford you love him. Flat out. Just say it. Here, like this." Laylee sat a little straighter, and she put on her serious face, which Skye guessed was supposed to look more like her. In a quiet but firm voice, she said, "By the way, Ford. I'm madly in love with you."

Skye snickered. "I couldn't."

Still in that mimicking way, Laylee added, "I think we should boot my sister out of our way and spend all our free time having wild, uninhibited sex."

"Ha!" Skye pushed her back on the bed, but she was laughing. "I'm not booting you out. You're welcome to stay here as long as you want. Move in. Permanently claim this room. In fact, I'm dubbing it Laylee's Lair. There. It's official." Before her sister could stop sputtering, Skye added, "I told Ford I was half in love with him, and he didn't mind."

"Didn't mind." Laylee scoffed, sitting up one more time. "I bet it rocked his world. And don't fib to the man. Tell him you love him madly, permanently. Forever more, amen."

"I'll consider it." Skye again took her hand. "If you promise me you'll stop talking about leaving."

There was no mistaking Laylee's cautious relief. "I'd actually love to stay." Her admiring gaze traveled around the room. "Your house is so you, and yet it suits me, too. The soothing colors and patterns, the . . . calm. I love it here, and I especially love being close to you."

"Good, then that's settled."

"I need to pay my own way—and I don't mean by doing a little grocery shopping or keeping an eye on the dogs, though I'm happy to do that, too." She bit her lip, then blurted, "I was thinking, if you and Ford work things out, and you decide to live with him, I'd buy this place from you."

Those words stole Skye's breath. She loved her house, but . . . The truth hit her: being at Ford's now felt like home, as well.

Laylee rushed into explanations. "If Ford doesn't work out, then it's his loss. Please, *please* don't think I'd want you to accept him just to make things easier for me. I'd gladly live in a tent with you, as long as you're happy. I swear. It's just that I can see how much you care for him, and it's so obvious that you're the one for him, so if you two make it permanent, and if you decide to live at his place, I'd be thrilled to buy your house." Laylee pressed her lips together and waited.

Daring to even imagine it, Skye whispered, "It would be awesome to live right next door to each other, wouldn't it?" Her relationship with her sister had gotten even closer with Ford around.

"Heck yeah, it would!" Laylee grabbed Skye, tugging her up from the bed and dancing her around the room, only drawing to a halt when Skye tripped. "Just so you know, Paul is working with me to help me get over my fear of Maybelline. He's an excellent teacher. I often join him on the dog walks. We're fast friends now, and he's been super patient."

They both heard the double knock on her back door, then the stampeding of dogs and the combined woofing of high and low voices. Ford called out, "Skye, everything okay?"

She smiled at Laylee, squeezed her in another hug, and dodging dogs, went out to the hall. "We're here, having a heart-to-heart."

Cautious, Ford approached Skye in the hall. A heart-to-heart? About what? he wondered.

"I saw your car still in the driveway and wondered if anything was wrong."

Skye grabbed him, planted a hot one on his lips, and then stated, "Our dogs need something different from us."

His heart lodged in his throat. He'd thought things were getting better. No, he and Skye didn't get enough alone time, but the situation was improving and with the fence done soon . . . Holding her closer, he asked, "What does that mean?"

She braced herself with a big breath. "They're going back and forth too much. It's confusing for them."

"Agreed." He had a solution for that, but before he could speak, she did.

"We could live together." Midnight eyes stared up at him earnestly. "Think about it. It'd be easier for us to coordinate who's walking them in the morning. It'll be easier for whichever of us gets home from work first."

She'd completely stolen his thunder, and now he couldn't stop smiling. "With Paul walking them each afternoon, that'd probably work."

Laylee stuck her head out of the bedroom. She held Tank more securely now because she'd learned her lesson, but surprisingly, she also seemed fine with Maybelline leaning into her side. "Hopefully, I'll still be around, too. I'm happy to let them in and out and to keep an eye on things."

Ford was speechless.

Skye gave him a blinding smile. "Who's moving? Me or you?"

It was an effort, but he dragged his gaze away from the sight of Laylee and both dogs. "Your sister seems to be a permanent fixture in your house, so how about mine?" And once she got comfortable there, he could move on to step two: a permanent commitment. That was what he wanted, but for Skye, he could bide his time.

"Perfect." She laced her arms around his neck. "It's working out, isn't it?"

"Good thing, because I'm not letting go. Not of Maybelline, or Tank." He put his forehead to hers. "Or you."

Her breath caught, and in the next second, she blurted, "I love you madly."

Jerking upright, he stared at her. "What did you say?"

From behind them, Laylee sang, "She loves you madly, permanently. Forever more, amen."

Getting a breath into his shocked lungs wasn't easy, but he finally managed it. "You mean it?"

Now with worry inching in, she said, "Yes, but that doesn't oblige you to—"

He lifted her off her feet, then crushed her close. Overwhelmed, thrilled, ready to shout, he said, "You love me."

Laylee laughed. "I told you so, sis."

Squeaking, Skye replied, "Don't pressure him."

Quickly, Ford set her back down. "I've loved you almost from the start." His hands shook a little as he cradled her face. "All my life, I wanted something, but no matter what I got, I kept on wanting. Great job, nice house, friends who are like family."

Softly, she covered one of his hands with her own. "I understand."

He knew she did, because she understood him. "Now, with you, and Maybelline . . ."

Laylee said, "And me?"

He half laughed, reached out an arm, and dragged her close. "Yeah, you, too."

She still held Tank but didn't seem to mind when Maybelline pressed her way into the middle of them. "My house is more wrecked than it's ever been," he went on, "but now it feels like a real home."

Skye's smile wobbled. "Oh, Ford."

"That's my cue to mosey on," Laylee whispered. She hugged her sister and kissed Ford on the cheek. "Love you both." Moving up the hall, she called out, "Who wants treats?" and both dogs started barking, Tank from her arms, and Maybelline in a mad race to catch up.

"She's getting a lot better."

Skye nodded. "She offered to buy my house."

His grin came slow and easy. "In that case, how would you feel about making things permanent?"

"Permanent?" Her gaze searched his.

"I love my house, so I'm glad we'll be living there, but it was never a home, and now I know why. It was missing you."

Her smile went crooked. "You're deliberately confusing me."

No, he was finally understanding. "A house is just a building. Different shapes, different sizes, but still, just structures. I could fill my house with nice furniture. Put on great music. Have the best entertainment center around."

"An immaculate yard," she added. "A trendy pool."

Now she was getting it, he thought. "They were just things to complement the structure."

"But a dog," she said. "Living and breathing, sharing and caring, that brought meaning?"

"Not just any dog, but the best dog. Maybelline is an enormous love-mutt." Her size was overshadowed only by her big heart and unending love. "She's been hurt."

Sad, Skye whispered, "It's unbearable if I dwell on it."

"Me, too. But she'll still accept any friendly hand. Someone treated her badly, and she's still so gentle."

"I'm glad she has us."

Us. The two of them together. "It's not just Maybelline that makes my house feel like a home, now. It's you. In ways I never imagined, you're my perfect counterpart. Beautiful and intelligent, understanding, friendly." His heart felt too big for his chest. "You know things about me that I've never told another soul."

Her lips quivered into a smile. "I love you."

He would never tire of hearing it. "We're going to have the very best life together."

"With Maybelline and Tank."

"And your sister next door."

She laughed.

"Will you marry me?" He touched his mouth to hers. "Today, or next month, or a year from now. Whenever you want, however you want."

"I want you." She hugged him. "When and where and how doesn't matter to me either, as long as we're together."

From the kitchen, Laylee shouted, "Then leave it all to me! I'll make it the best wedding ever!"

Together—all three of them, with barking dogs joining in—they laughed.

*Two Months Later*

"My sister is brilliant."

Ford couldn't disagree. For weeks, Laylee had grilled them both on things they liked so that she could put together an ideal wedding—for them. He had to say, it suited them perfectly.

Casual and relaxed—just as Skye had requested—the ceremony had taken place in the combined backyards where his friends, *his family*, could gather and all their animals could safely play.

And his wife . . . her guests included fifty or so of her and Laylee's relatives, who were every bit as nice as his wife and sister-in-law. It took both properties to hold them all, but he couldn't have been happier.

Skye was now his wife, and God, he loved her. "You're stunning," he whispered, carefully gathering her close again. The material of her dress seemed fragile to him, all white froth magically drifting around her ankles, but leaving her shoulders and back bare.

Laylee flitted by, going from one house to the next, seeing to their guests and the dogs with equal attention.

Knox, Bray and Marcus strode up, all of them smiling at him. While they chatted, Knox tracked Laylee's every move.

Ford nudged him. "As the best man, you could offer the maid of honor some help."

Without taking his gaze off Laylee, he said, "Already did, but she refused. Says she has everything in hand."

Paul joined them, only to heckle Knox. "You're hopeless." He physically turned his friend, took his drink from his hand, and gave him a light shove. "Go, don't ask, just start helping."

Skeptical, Knox glared at him. "You're sure that won't irritate her?"

Skye whispered, "I'm pretty sure it will."

"Shh," Ford said, amused. Then louder, "Trust Paul. He's her buddy now."

With a roll of his eyes, Knox started forward, but growled to Paul, "If you're wrong, I'm going to kick your ass."

Paul grinned, then reassured everyone by saying, "He's joking."

Marcus and Bray just lifted their brows.

Frowning, Paul muttered, "He better be joking." Then he took off to follow Knox.

Marcus pulled her into a hug. "In case I haven't said it, welcome to the family."

Bray got her next. "Ford is a brother, whether we're blood related or not. So that makes you a sister."

"Well," she said, "I already adore you all. Plus my family loved Ford on sight."

Ford glanced over to where her relatives lounged on lawn furniture beneath a shade tree, all of them fawning over Maybelline. His dog loved it. "I'm pretty damn happy with them, too."

All around him, chaos reigned. Tank ran with the other dogs, and even Lucy's cat was in attendance, sprawled on her lap while she talked with Skye's cousins.

Dog fur clung to most of his furniture—and his black wedding slacks.

He and Skye constantly worked with the animals, reassuring them, loving them, teaching them better habits.

And every night, she slept in his arms.

Together, they'd created the perfect life for them.

Together, they had a home.

*Force of Nature*

MAISEY YATES

# Chapter 1

The puppy-dog eyes were a little much. Remington Lane—Remy to his friend; he only had the one—stared down at the most pathetic, beseeching expression he had ever seen in his life.

The eyes were pitiful, large and dewy. Their owner straight from the shelter by the looks of things and trying hard to tug on heartstrings Remy wasn't even sure he had.

And then he noticed the dog.

The dog seemed unbothered; however, his one and only friend's little sister, Lydia Clay, seemed terribly bothered, and tragic on top of it, standing in his doorway on the verge of begging.

"I couldn't leave him in the shelter, not after I saw who he had belonged to," she said, the emotion in her large eyes intensifying as she gazed up at him.

The *he* in question was the most sorry heap of bones Remy had ever seen. An ancient-looking cow dog that had neither bark nor bite.

He felt pained by what he expected to come next. Lydia was doing her best to *look* pained.

"Who did he belong to?" he asked, already sure he knew the answer and not liking it one bit.

"Your dad. He was your dad's dog, Remy."

Lydia might as well have hauled off and punched him in the gut. Because if there was one thing Remy didn't care about, it was his dad. Well, if there were two things he didn't care about, it was his dad and where the man's soul had ended up after his demise.

Hunter Lane, *gone too late*, quite honestly.

"Of course that was my dad's dog. He looks halfway to death's door, and like no one has ever bothered to take an interest in him." Remy did his best to steel himself against any sympathy the dog's fate might arouse within him.

Lydia looked up at him, pleading now, her hands clasped at the center of her chest.

Lordy. He did not have time for this. But if there was one thing he did care about, it was the Clay family. How could he not?

His own family was, well, the technical term was . . . a shit show.

His dad had been an evil drunk, and his mom had been too busy spreading herself around town to pay any mind to her only son. Remy had spent his childhood going back and forth between the room his mother rented over the bar in town, and squatting in a bedroom in his dad's barely habitable ranch house.

The Clay family had been his real family. They had practically raised him. They had taken care of him. They were . . . good people in a world that had left Remy uncertain whether anyone could be trusted.

But the problem with good people was that they were too soft. Lydia was a perfect example. Remy and Lydia's older brother, Matthew, had been friends ever since sixth grade. Lydia had been an irritating fourth-grader back then, wandering around with her blond hair up in an absurd ponytail, saving baby birds, snakes, and any other critters who crossed her path. Some would argue that many of them didn't even need saving; they had just encountered an overenthusiastic child with a savior complex.

He had in fact tried to argue that point with her on a couple of occasions, but most especially when she had brought a raccoon home from an abandoned nest when she was seventeen years old. That fat-ass raccoon was still alive, and—in spite of Lydia's best efforts to return it to the wild—living in her house, and eating better than most people.

Remy resented it.

The trouble was, he couldn't quite resent Lydia. However much he might want to.

She was sweet and good, and there were too few things in this world that were sweet and good besides.

She was the real deal in a way he'd never been, that was for damn sure. His version of good was not causing harm. He'd gone out of his way to make a life that was self-contained and didn't cause any trouble. He tried to build more than he broke—that was his goal.

As a rancher, he tried to take care of his animals and honor their use—yes, he ranched beef, but he took the duties of his work seriously and to heart. As a programmer he tried to combine the useful and the entertaining—as a kid he'd been fascinated by the way things were put together.

Whether it was an engine in a car or the invisible building blocks of the video games he played at the Clay house, he always wanted to know how things worked and why.

Maybe it was a side effect of being a kid in a house that he couldn't make heads or tails of, but whatever the reason, that fascination had taken him places. He wasn't saving the world or anything like that, but he hoped his personal scales would balance in the end.

Lydia wasn't just neutral though. She wasn't balancing scales.

She seemed to think any animal with a limp was her problem to solve.

He wondered sometimes if that was why she took an interest in him—her whole family, really.

They were a constant presence in his life—he'd had dinner with the Clay family the other night. They always included him in their get-togethers.

But much like the pathetic dog at Lydia's side, he was a shelter animal. Not a pedigreed anything.

"Looks like you have yourself another dog, tiger," he said, moving to close the front door of his house.

"No," she said, stopping him from shutting the door, her blue eyes stormy. "I can't take him. I mean, I actually tried. But he and Pascal took an instant loathing to each other. Also, Maleficent can't handle large dogs without a lot of preparation and coaching, not after the incident with those pit bulls at her previous owner's house."

He pinched the bridge of his nose. "So let me get this straight. This dog is here because he and a raccoon had a personality clash, and your Chihuahua mix has a Napoleon complex."

"She has complex post-traumatic stress disorder."

"She's a Chihuahua," he said. "Her brain is the size of a walnut. Nothing in there is complex."

Lydia sniffed, her indignation clear in every fiber of her being. "I'm going to choose to ignore that, because I assume that you're grieving, and therefore in a little bit of a dark space."

"You would assume incorrectly. I drank a six-pack of Bud Light and shot off fireworks the night my dad died."

"It isn't Hank's fault that your dad was a terrible father."

"No, it's not," Remy said. "It's also not my fault. Not my fault that he owned a dog that he didn't take care of and didn't have succession planning for. I'm just grateful that the dog isn't me."

As soon as he said that, the dog looked up at him. Made eye contact. And Remy felt . . . seen. Scolded.

That dog looked him dead in the face and asked without words: *But you're okay with it being me? That's a fine thing.*

"It's a no-kill shelter that you work at, right?"

"Yes," she said. "But old dogs like him are difficult to place. Can you at least . . . consider fostering him? He just got uprooted from his home, and I don't know if he's the best pet because I suspect he's endured some years of neglect."

Well, Remy was dead familiar with that. He hadn't asked to be born any more than the dog had asked to be bought by his dad and brought into that house. It was so damned annoying. That he felt sorry for the dog. That he felt kinship with the dog.

"This is—"

"You have plenty of land. Your house is big." She clasped her hands again and looked up at him, like a sad little orphan, and he was of the mind that if he said no, he was going to come across as a total monster.

He didn't *always* mind that. Honestly. He didn't have a reputation for being the friendliest man around town. Though his reserve stemmed from the fact that people often weren't all that friendly to him—his dad's reputation preceded him.

But the Clay family gave a shit about him. And as a result, he felt obliged to give more than a shit about them.

"I don't know anything about taking care of a dog. I don't have any supplies."

"Lucky for you, I know everything about taking care of animals. And I'm going to be here to help you. Every step of the way."

# Chapter 2

Lydia Clay had an affinity for difficult animals. It was her great tragedy that one of the difficult animals she had the greatest affinity for was Remington Lane.

Talk about pointless crushes. She'd been nursing one for him for so many years that she had forgotten what it was like to live without the terrible, aching feeling in her chest. But of course, she was the target audience for his particular kind of lost and abandoned.

She could remember her parents staying up late at night talking about what to do with Remy.

They had known pretty quickly after Matthew had developed a friendship with him that not everything was okay in his home. Quite the opposite.

And they had done a lot of soul-searching on that subject.

She could remember the point, when Matthew and Remy had been sophomores in high school, that her parents had finally decided they were going to have to ask if Remy could move in.

He was often dirty, his clothing ill fitting, and he was terribly, obviously neglected.

His parents hadn't minded where he lived; in fact, they had seemed relieved by the Clays' offer. Her parents had taken him in, and they had helped him get on the path to college.

Lydia had died many deaths because it was both exhilarating and debilitating to have the boy she had a crush on living in her house.

The chance of running into him in the hall in the morning or at night had been a fearsome thing.

She was two years younger than Remy, and during the time they'd lived together—starting when she was fourteen and he was sixteen—she would come to know she would never have a chance with him. She was just his friend's kid sister.

That realization hadn't stopped her fervent fantasies about him, sadly.

Yet he'd never looked at her that way, not even one time.

She'd thought maybe he would need her family forever, but no.

Remy was good with computers. He had created something she still could hardly understand, some interface that was used on a whole bunch of popular social media sites, and he had cashed out when he was twenty-five, bought himself a ranch, and she wasn't even sure if he did anything other than run it now.

It was rumored that the deal had been worth multiple millions of dollars, not that you would know it by the way he lived.

He definitely had a nice truck, and a nice pair of boots. His house was modest in size, though beautifully designed.

It was a funny thing, that Remy had gotten into ranching. At least, she had always thought so. Because his dad had been a rancher, and Remy had never seemed to have much of anything but disdain for his dad.

He approached ranching very differently, though. Maybe in part because he had ample funds. But . . .

This was why she thought he would actually be great for Hank.

"Can Hank and I come in?" she asked.

He treated her to a cold blue side eye that made her heart race.

This was her problem. She always liked the difficult ones.

If somebody said that a horse was untrained, she wanted to train it. If somebody said that a dog was so traumatized it could never be a pet, she wanted to teach that dog that it could trust humans after all.

Yet another connection with Remy.

"Come on in," he said, relenting. She gently pulled Hank's leash, and the two of them entered Remy's domain.

She had been around Remy for the greater part of her life, and still, sometimes she forgot how tall he was. She barely came to the middle of his chest.

He looked down at the dog, an expression of pain on his handsome face. "Does he have vermin?"

"He does not have vermin. He's a very respectable gentleman."

"Says the woman who lives with a rodent."

"I live with *several* rodents, Remington. I think you know that."

"I didn't, actually. Thank you for confirming."

"Well, once I nurse the vole back to health . . ."

He threw his hands up. "What the hell are you doing that for? I have never heard of such a thing."

"I rehabilitate animals. It's what I do."

"People don't rehabilitate rodents. They catch them in traps. Occasionally stomp them."

She sputtered. "Well, I don't." She knew that Remy was being intentionally difficult. Because he often was. "I'm sorry that your relationship with your dad was unhappy. I really am. But . . . this dog is just another of his victims. The same as you."

"Well, I'm not a dog, though."

"Granted," she said. She took a deep breath. "I'm going to help you. With the dog. I'll come over every day." Just saying that made her heart rate pick up. So much exposure to Remy might be dangerous to her heart.

"Sure. Fine. But I . . . What am I supposed to do with him in the meantime?"

"Do you have a crate or anything?"

"I don't have any animals in my house."

"That's very strange," she said.

"It's really not."

She sighed. "Okay. Why don't you and Hank come to my place. And then we'll get some supplies for his first night."

"Why didn't you just bring them?"

"I didn't know if you were going to take him." Except, she kind of had. Because the thing about Remy was that he might pretend he was tough, a completely impenetrable fortress, but she knew there was more to him than that.

"All right. I'll . . ."

"I'll drive—you can take Hank in your truck."

"He's a dog I don't know."

"You're going to get to know him."

# Chapter 3

After he got the mutt loaded up into his front seat, he started the engine and began to follow Lydia out of the driveway. He punched the call button of his phone on the console of his truck.

"Matthew," he said. "Your sister just brought a dog to my house."

His best friend sighed. "That sounds like her. Why isn't she keeping it?"

"Because he belonged to my old man."

He heard his friend's breath hiss through his teeth. "Well, she misread that situation."

"And how."

Except he did have the dog, so had she misread the situation, or did she have his number in more ways than he wanted to admit?

The thing about Lydia was . . . she was special.

Matthew was his best friend, and his parents were the only people even close to parental figures he'd ever had.

Lydia was something else altogether. She'd always had the

power to make him laugh, to make him smile. To make him sigh in horror, also, when she did things like save baby mice from certain doom.

He could remember that well. She'd had a whole passel of the little beasts in a basket, wrapped in towels.

*Those things are disgusting.*

*They're living creatures, Remy!*

*Aren't you at least going to bathe them?*

*That's the dumbest thing I've ever heard. They're tiny! They'd die!*

Lydia Clay, telling him he was dumb about animals for more than a decade.

"I'm on my way to her place to get supplies for the dog. The dog that is sitting in the front seat of my new truck."

"Well. If you weren't such a fancy-pants, it wouldn't bother you that the dog was in your truck."

Remy winced. He did not like to think of himself as a fancy-pants. But the truth was, he lived comfortably, and he liked the things he had. He had grown up in scarcity, and that had been shit.

He hadn't had any control over the things surrounding him, and now he did. He'd built his house from the ground up and chosen everything inside it. He'd bought a brand-new truck that only he had ever driven.

His reaction to feeling out of control as a kid was normal. He'd read that on a *Psychology Today* blog post.

It was normal, so that meant he didn't have to do anything to fix it.

He had decided to become a rancher because it was almost . . . revenge. Getting back at his father just a little bit for the way he had acted—as if ranch life required they live in a wallow.

And yeah, being a little bit of a programming genius—or in all honesty, programming lucky—had given him a boost up in life.

It freed him up to work the ranch. He still used his degree. He programmed games for fun and didn't really need them to earn a whole lot. He didn't need the ranch to earn a whole lot. He had the best of all possible worlds. Plenty to keep him busy, but the stakes were low.

He had won at life, basically. And his dad was dead. Yay for him. Except now, suddenly there was the dog.

"Your husband likes my truck," Remy said.

"I know he does. I give thanks every day that he's not your type. Because he would've left me for you a long time ago."

Remy laughed. "Yeah. The whole commitment thing's not for me."

"Why not?"

"You know why not. Family is a difficult, thorny thing in my opinion. And I don't want much of anything to do with it."

"You like my family well enough."

"I do. And when you and Jackson have babies, I'm happy to be their fun uncle who gives them back to you the minute they start to cry."

This was a well-worn conversation between himself and Matthew. Matthew thought that Remy should want what he had. Someone to care about him. Someone to go home to at night.

But Remy just didn't see any of that leading to happiness.

Yeah, Matthew's family was great. They always had been. His parents loved their kids, not in spite of who they were, but because of it. They seemed to enjoy watching their children come into their own, and they had let Remy know they were proud of him too. But Remy couldn't imagine being that lucky in life himself.

In some ways, he had outrun his past. Financially. He was more successful than he had ever imagined he could be. But personally?

Work hard, play hard. That was his motto. But coastal Oregon was pretty rural, and small towns meant too many people he had to see all the time if he wanted to have one-night stands that really stayed one night, and didn't devolve into him running into the person at the feed store.

He often drove out of Myrtle Creek and into Coos Bay to hook up. Spending a little bit of time by the ocean, eating fresh seafood and picking up women who wouldn't track him down the next day, that was his idea of a good time.

"Well, we're almost at Lydia's place. So I have to go face her rodents."

"A raccoon isn't a rodent," Matthew said.

"Thank you, I'm aware of that. She has a vole too."

"What?"

"Yeah. Voles, plural actually. That's your sister. It's a mystery to me why you don't get on her about marrying up. Maybe because no man wants to move in with critters."

He hung up the phone and got out of the truck. He assumed that the dog needed to stay inside. He frowned. The dog better not tear up the front seat of that truck. . . .

"How was he?" Lydia asked.

"Your brother?"

She laughed. "What? No. The dog."

"Oh. Right. I was just talking to your brother on the phone. The dog was fine."

"Oh, good. I'll just keep . . ."

She was fussing around, moving buckets out of the way, so he took stock of the place. The little cottage that Lydia called home was ramshackle at best. It was situated half a mile up a dirt road, and back behind some trees.

She had a chicken coop out front, and a hutch of some kind. When he peered closer, he saw that there were rabbits in it.

He liked animals, well enough. But he liked them to have a

purpose. Lydia seemed to have a surplus of pointless animals, and he could not for the life of him understand that.

"Just come in for a second. I have several bags of dog food, but I need to find the formula for older canines. And I do have leashes, collars, crates. I have stuff so you can give him a bath. . . ."

"Don't dogs clean themselves?"

"That's cats."

"I have to give him a bath?"

"When he's dirty." She looked at him as if he was an idiot. Which was a novel experience. People around town might be a little suspect of him, but they knew he was smart.

In his opinion, smart was a many-headed beast. There was tech smart, which he was, he couldn't deny. He'd also been given a lot of help. Without the Clays' guidance, he would never have gotten himself to college, and he wouldn't have had access to the technology that had made his success possible.

He would never have made the necessary connections; he would never have even known what careers were available to him. For a minute there he'd thought he'd move away. That his whole life would be in tech. But he hadn't much liked the idea of moving to a city.

Part of him had always felt most at home on a ranch.

It had been weird living in the beautiful cul-de-sac home with Lydia's family. Weird to have a small yard and a pool, a paved driveway.

Of course, he also hadn't expected to program a template in his third year of college that was foundational to every relevant social media site and was still being built off today.

When he'd been offered an obscene amount of money to sell it, he'd taken it.

That had given him something even better than a new life. It had given him the freedom to live whatever the hell life he wanted.

So yeah, he was smart.

Though there were a few things that baffled him still. In the top tier were families and why the hell people chose to start them.

Matthew and Jackson were happy, and he loved that for them. But commitment was never going to be for him.

Remy followed Lydia up the paved path, and through the bright red front door, which had a cheerful yellow flower wreath hanging on it.

It was so very her.

Simple but with thoughtful details that were there just because.

That was one of the things about Lydia that fascinated him. She wasn't intense, she wasn't on a trajectory. She didn't seem to be proving anything to anyone.

She was just living.

The house was all natural wood inside, but the first thing he noticed was not any of the cute décor. It was the raccoon on the kitchen counter.

"Hello," Lydia said in her best baby voice. "It is so good to see you, Pascal."

Pascal wobbled across the counter toward them.

Then he stood on his hind legs and lifted his front feet up.

Remy felt his lip curl against his will.

"You don't like him?" Lydia asked.

"I find it . . . It's a lot, Lydia."

"Well. It's not your problem."

She turned away, and her blond hair swung with the motion. Just as the sun came through the kitchen window and illuminated her profile. He felt a tug of fondness in his chest. For this girl he had known all his life.

It reminded him why he was doing this.

The light shifted just slightly, and the blue of her eyes became more intense. A little bit of color flooded her cheeks. She smiled. Her mouth was softer than he had remembered, and it was as if the word *girl* shifted right out of his brain, and the word *woman* took its place.

*Oh hell.*

He blinked. "Where's the stuff? And you said something about a crate. Because I really can't have him running around the place at night."

She snorted. "I don't think Hank is going to run around anywhere. But it's not a bad idea to see if he's crate trained. I don't think your dad had him inside the house at all."

"So he isn't house-trained?"

"Probably not. There were a lot of animals at your dad's place. They were all in pretty rough shape."

Guilt kicked him square in the chest, and he didn't know why it should. Whatever the fuck his dad had been up to had nothing to do with him. He hadn't had any contact with him. Distance was a necessary part of surviving the Hunter Lane experience.

"What happened to them?"

"The horses are at a sanctuary."

"I would've been a better bet for the horses," he said. "At least I know what to do with them."

"Some of them had to be euthanized." She said it very softly, tears filling her eyes.

He felt regret. Rage. Because nobody should treat fine animals that way. And yes, he had a difficult time understanding why people wanted their house full of animals, but there was no question in his mind that if you consented to take care of an animal, then that was an agreement you made with the earth itself. Violating it . . .

That was why his dad had found an early grave, frankly.

Because how dare you put animals in a cage, where they couldn't even take care of themselves, and let them suffer?

"He's a bastard for that," he said.

"He's a bastard for a lot of things," she said.

"No argument from me."

"I can check on some of the other horses and see . . . if you'd like them."

"Yeah. I'd like you to do that. He shouldn't have been allowed to have animals. Or kids, frankly."

"I know growing up with him wasn't a great experience."

"Not in the least."

"Well. I'll just get your stuff and then you can . . . You can go."

"Thanks, Lydia." And for the first time he meant it. Because yeah, he didn't know what to do with the dog, but finding out that there had been other animals at the place, finding out that his dad had been up to the same awful shit he had always been up to . . . now Remy couldn't walk away.

That made him feel a hell of a lot more like he needed to get himself involved. He had questioned his decision at first. He hadn't known what in hell he ought to do.

He had agreed to foster the dog simply out of obligation to Lydia and her family.

But . . . there was more to it than that. His dad had been a terrible man, and Remy didn't plan on continuing his bloodline. Not ever.

Remy had already made his legacy, thanks to some of the work he'd done in programming. And he was working at making a legacy of his ranch. But some of his duty was going to have to come back to taking care of the animals that his dad had left to die.

It was his burden now. He hadn't chosen it, just as he hadn't chosen to be his father's son.

"All right, I just need to go in the back—"

"Where in the back?"

"Just my utility room."

"I'll go with you."

She nodded. Her house was tidy, but it couldn't be called spotless. It was definitely the domain of animals. There were three dogs lying on little beds, and their tails thumped when he walked past.

Those dogs didn't even know him, yet they seemed happy to see him.

Suddenly his throat felt tight.

They went down the hall, and she opened up the back door. There was a neat utility room, filled with different bags of feed, leashes hanging on pegs, and multiple kennels.

"This one on the top shelf," she indicated, starting to reach upward.

"Don't do that," he said. "I've got it."

He moved in front of her and reached past her, grabbing hold of one of the kennels. Then he turned, and that brought them just so they were about an inch apart. She was looking up at him, and for some reason, he noticed for the very first time that Lydia Clay had freckles sprinkled across her nose.

She smelled like wildflowers, vanilla, and something even more delicate.

And her cheeks turned bright red.

The shade of red cheeks turned for one reason and one reason only.

Lord Almighty.

He backed up, tucked the crate underneath his arm, and turned away from her.

"Well. That ought to do it."

He could hear her expel a large breath. "Yes," she said. "That should do it."

"I'll . . . I'll give you a heads-up in the morning to let you know how we did."

"Thanks. I really do appreciate it."

"And if you can get the information about the horses . . ."

"I will."

"Thanks . . . thanks for bringing him to me, Lydia."

And with that, he turned and walked out of the house. When he got outside, he felt as if he had dodged a bullet, and he couldn't quite say why.

# Chapter 4

Lydia couldn't sleep. She was sitting in the center of her bed, picking at a fingernail. She was on edge after that encounter with Remy. After he had thanked her. Thanked her for bringing the dog, thanked her for involving him.

He had gone from resentful to thankful a lot quicker than she ever could have imagined. And then, there had been that moment in the utility room.

**HEAR THAT YOU HAVE VOLES.**

The text from her brother was overdramatic on arrival.

**Voles that I rescued. I don't have an infestation.**

**It's weird.**

**I'm weird.**

That was true. No one could ever dispute it, and no one ever had. Lydia Clay was a weirdo. Maybe that was why she had always felt an affinity with Remy. Not that he would ever identify as a weirdo. Hell, he was one of the most beautiful men she had ever seen, and that wasn't just a personal opinion or her own bias. He was over six feet tall, broad and muscular. His angular jaw was just the kind of sharp that caught a woman's eye, his eyes a piercing blue, his nose straight, his mouth beguiling.

Yes. She had used the word *beguiling*. It was just that. There was no other word for it.

She would give quite a few things to be less weird, and less obsessed with him. Sometimes she wondered if she had imprinted on him like a baby deer. Maybe that was her problem.

Oh well. She wasn't going to dwell on her obsession. Because there was no point in dwelling. There was no point in anything but helping him with Hank.

She didn't think about Remy all the time.

Just when she had to deal with him. And that was . . . often. He came to every family function, after all. She sighed and lay on her back on the bed, arms out like a starfish. And when she woke up the next morning, she put her animal shelter T-shirt on, a pair of jeans and sneakers, and went to work. Work started first at home. Feeding the animals, checking in on Chicken Little, her one-footed banty hen, and giving kibble to all the pets that needed kibble, including Terrence the blind ferret.

Some of them required special medications as well. Then she went to the shelter for the day. An elderly couple came to look at small dogs, and they left with a geriatric Chiweenie.

It always made Lydia's heart feel full to bursting when an animal found its people. And what she loved about the shelter was that it facilitated people finding exactly the right dogs for them. So many of the dogs that came into the shelter were older, dogs who had lost their owners because they had passed away or they had had to go into assisted living.

In most cases, those dogs had been very well taken care of. Hank's situation was unusual.

With Hank on her mind, she called the equine rescue and asked for an update about the three surviving horses she had brought in.

"I know someone who's willing to take them and care for them. Give them a permanent home."

"They should be ready in another week," said Shelley, her contact at the rescue.

"Great. I'll give him that timeframe."

She didn't mention that Remy was Hunter's son. She didn't think he needed anyone wondering about his character. She thought so often about small-town gossip and how damaging it could be to have parents with difficult reputations, because she had seen it affect Remy. In spite of the fact that he had never been anything but good, disciplined, successful.

The opposite of his parents in all ways.

He had done well for himself, and still, he seemed to exist on the fringes everywhere but in the Clay household.

She wrinkled her nose, and went through some new intake paperwork, scheduling vaccinations and neutering appointments with the three veterinarians who volunteered to work on the shelter animals.

Then she texted Remy to let him know that she was on her way, and tried to tamp down the little flutter in her stomach.

He didn't text back, but she drove straight to his place all the same. When she arrived, his truck wasn't in the driveway, and she felt a kick of irritation.

She walked up the front steps to the house and peered in the window. If the dog had been left there alone, she was going to be annoyed at Remy.

What if Hank was in a kennel? She didn't think Remy was unkind to animals. If he were, she would never have developed a fixation on him no matter how sexy he was. Rodents before bro-dents. That was her motto.

But he was an inexperienced dog owner by his own admission, so it was possible he just didn't know what to do with Hank during the day.

She heard a motor rumbling and the sound of tires on gravel, and she turned to see his shiny red truck barreling up the road. And there was Hank, sitting proudly in the passenger seat, tongue hanging out. His shaggy brown fur looked glossy, even from where Lydia was standing. Had Remy brushed him?

She blinked. She could hardly believe it. And then she took note of the man himself. He was wearing a cowboy hat, grinning, singing along to the radio.

It took him a second to notice her. When he did, his expression went blank, and he pulled up beside her car, killing the engine and getting out of the driver's seat.

"Didn't expect you this early."

"I did send you a text. The shelter is only open until four on Tuesdays."

"I see."

He rounded the front of the truck and went to the passenger side, then opened the door up. She half expected Hank to leap out. But instead Remy reached inside and picked the dog up, placing him gingerly on the ground. She blinked. "So, things are going well."

"Yeah. I think so."

"Yesterday, you seemed so . . . down on it."

"I'm down on anything pertaining to my dad."

He walked past her, and she was surprised to see Hank follow at the edge of his boot heel, as if he was superglued to him. No leash required.

She had just been thinking what an amazing thing it was that the shelter allowed people to find animals that matched their needs perfectly. But apparently, Remy had found his perfect match in Hank. They were like long-lost soulmates, and she wasn't sure if she had ever seen anything quite like that. She followed him up the front porch steps and into the house. Hank went straight into the living room and jumped up onto the leather couch, causing the throw on the back of it to slide down and cover him. He rested his chin on his front paws and looked utterly at home and satisfied.

Remy crossed his arms and pushed his cowboy hat up. "I

thought we had a chat about that, Hank. I am unsure about you being on the furniture."

Lydia chuckled. "I think you've lost that battle."

"Maybe," he said.

"I talked to Shelley at the equine rescue. She said that the three horses should be ready to move to a nonmedical facility in about a week. They're doing well."

He nodded. "I have plenty of room."

"Do you have use for three more horses?"

"I don't need to have use for them. They can stand out in the field and live the rest of their lives happy and well fed." He grimaced. "Listen, Lydia, I admit that I'm not the bleeding heart about animals that you are. But my dad wasn't a good man. He treated everybody that came into his life—man or beast—like they were there to serve him. And if they didn't serve him, they didn't matter. If I can do even one thing to counteract some of that . . . to take away some of the harm, I want to do it. I can't change the way people see me, I can't do anything about whatever reputation I've ended up with around town by virtue of the fact that I'm related to Hunter Lane and Cassie Elliott, but I can try to do good all on my own. If no one ever sees it . . . that doesn't matter. I've done alright for myself."

It was a beautiful thing to say, but it made Lydia feel profoundly sad. "But you deserve to be seen for who you are. You deserve for people to realize that you're a good man."

"It's not about deserving anything," he said. "Leastways not from my perspective. I don't mind. I have my house up here, I have my ranch . . . I don't need recognition."

"Don't you want it?"

"Not especially. I've never really seen the need. It just doesn't matter overly much to me. I don't have plans to start a happy family here."

"Why not?"

"Because I think that kind of thing is for other people. People who grew up with a different kind of life. People who . . . people who had it just a little bit different."

"My family loves you," she said.

*I love you.*

The words welled up deep and true inside her. There was a reason she had never been in a serious relationship with anyone else. There was a reason that although she had gone out with a couple of men a couple of different times, it had never gone past a chaste kiss at the door.

There was a reason that at twenty-seven, she was still a virgin, and not the born-again kind, the original variety.

She had decided to devote her life to animals. To nature. She had decided that she was going to give her all to it. Some people devoted their lives to the church. She devoted hers to the care and keeping of critters. And her parents had accepted that. They understood that she wasn't ambitious, that she would only ever be able to afford to rent a little house at the end of a dirt road. She had accepted that too. But what she hadn't fully accepted was that her feelings for Remy were tied up in all her life choices.

They were stronger than she would like to believe. But it was more than just being attracted to her older brother's gorgeous best friend, who had been part of her family for so many years. She now realized it was love.

"And I'm damned appreciative of your family," he said. "They've been everything. They mean the world to me. But I don't need the whole town to look at me and see a good person."

"What do you need?"

He shrugged. "I expect that I have it. My house, being a rancher. My dad is gone. So, that's a boon."

"Now you even have a dog," she said.

"Yeah," he said.

And yet she could feel that there was a sadness to him. As if there was something missing, something he couldn't articulate.

She knew because she felt the same way. She had a pretty good life. But sometimes . . .

Sometimes she wondered if she was missing out. Sometimes she wondered if she needed . . .

"What?" he asked, as if he could read her thoughts.

"Nothing."

She told herself Remy was a dead end. That was the honest truth. And while she was standing there grappling with the hard reality of her feelings for him, she also tried to grab hold of that one and clutch it tightly.

Did she just want to live in a house with her animals forever? Did she want to be consecrated to the church of animal rescue? It wasn't something she had really put into words before, so it wasn't something that she had really accepted.

Her heart was in a holding pattern. For Remy.

But the man had a pretty complete life.

"Matthew thinks I should want what he has," Remy said.

"And you don't?"

The corner of his mouth lifted upward. "Not in the market for a husband, no."

She rolled her eyes. "Right, but a wife."

"Not really in the market for one of those either. Because I've never seen marriage pan out for members of my family."

"My parents are very stable."

"Yes, they are. Your parents are wonderful people. I don't think I've ever seen a parent support kids the way yours do. And it spilled over onto me, and for that I'm damn grateful. Trust me on that. But it doesn't mean I would know the first thing about how to have a relationship. Although I do know about other aspects of romance."

The way he said it, all throaty and serious, made her feel warm.

"Well. How nice for you."

"That's why Matthew was such a great wingman for me, and

I was such a great one to him. We were both very charming and not competing for the same type."

"Must be a big loss, not having your wingman."

He lifted a brow. "I do okay."

That made her feel hot in ways she wished it didn't. Women had always liked him. Even before he'd become so successful. How could they not like him?

"I think we should give Hank a bath," she said, eager to change the subject.

"I sprayed some air freshener in the truck," he said.

She rolled her eyes. "We bathed him at the shelter but he was a mess, and I think it would be a good idea to get him all cleaned up here so you can get accustomed to the process."

"You've handed me extra chores, Lydia, and I'm not sure how I feel about it."

"But, Remington, it's a chore that will love you back."

Remy grumbled as he walked past her down the hall toward the bathroom, but she heard the water start to run, and she laughed.

But then Hank heard it too and bolted, straight off the couch and right out of the room.

# Chapter 5

Remy came out of the bathroom to find Lydia standing there looking lost, and no dog in sight. "What just happened?"

"I don't think Hank wants a bath."

"Well, I don't know that I need to give him one. . . ."

"He clearly has a fear of baths! But we can work on that."

"You don't know for sure? Didn't you give him a bath at the shelter?"

"Not me personally. It happened before I got there for the day. That was before anyone knew whose dog he was."

"Where did he go?"

"Into your . . . your bedroom," she said.

Her words faltered a little bit there, but he didn't analyze her hesitation. Instead, he turned and made his way toward his bedroom. Where there was no dog in sight.

Then he heard a pitiful whining coming from underneath the bed.

There was something about the sound that gripped him fully in the chest. Something about it that reminded him of being a child. A powerless being who didn't understand what the person in charge was going to do, or why they were going to do it. Being a child was a lot like being a dog, he supposed. You were dependent on the people who were supposedly caring for you to make good decisions, and once it had been proven that they weren't going to make reasonable decisions nine times out of ten, it just became difficult to trust. He knew that as well as he knew anything. He'd never thought that he would relate to an old cow dog. But right now, he did. And then some.

"Could you go get some cheese out of my fridge?" he asked.

"Sure," Lydia said, and he heard her footsteps disappearing down the hallway.

"I don't mean you any harm," he said. "Remember we had a good day. And I'm not one of those people who flips on a dime, who acts happy with you one moment and then gets angry the next. I know my dad was like that. Probably got you because he figured you'd be of some use to him in some way, but then you never quite did what he wanted you to. That was me too. He wanted a son, but not me. And actually, I'm okay with that. Because why the hell would I want to be a good son to a man like him? You don't want to be a chip off the old block when the block is nothing more than rotten wood. But I can take my time and earn your trust if I need to."

"I've got it," came a soft voice from behind him. Lydia had returned without his noticing. She swept into the room and knelt down beside him, cheese in hand. But it wasn't cheese that he could smell. It was her. Some concoction of lilacs and vanilla. She had worn that perfume for a long time. It was actually a deeply embedded memory, but he'd never really thought about it until that moment. Or maybe, it hadn't been significant until that moment. Lydia was a constant, one he could admit he took for granted in some ways. But right now, he wasn't taking her for granted at all. She felt significant and singular, and unexpected in a way he couldn't quite put his finger on.

She handed him a little cube of cheese, and he took it, extending his hand beneath the bed. There was no movement.

"Poor guy," she said.

"Yeah," he agreed.

He waited. And then, finally, Hank's brown nose surged forward. And Remy watched as the dog belly-crawled toward the cheese, sniffing at it suspiciously.

"I'm sorry," he said. "Because I'm definitely using this to bait you into a bath."

The dog emerged, and took a bit of the cheese. Eventually, he came out entirely, climbing onto Remy's lap, and sitting there, as if he wasn't far too large for such a thing.

Remy sat, patting him on the side. "It's okay," he said. "Well. Now I feel like anything I do is going to be a betrayal."

"It's okay," she said. "It won't be."

"Says you. He might feel differently."

"But when it's over, and he's fine, then he'll know that this is okay, and next time will be easier. Maybe not easy, but definitely easier."

Following his instincts, instincts he wasn't quite sure he could trust, Remy stood, holding the big dog in his arms. Hank leaned against him, resting his head on Remy's shoulder like a big baby. And Remy held him fast. "It's all right," he said.

He carried the dog down the hall toward the bathroom, where the water was still running. And to his credit, Hank didn't freak out, so Remy felt he must be doing something right.

Then slowly, very slowly he began to lower Hank into the bath.

And as soon as Hank's feet touched the surface, he began to kick. And a wave of water splashed over Remy and Lydia.

He lifted Hank back up. "It's okay. It's okay."

The dog panted and whimpered. Remy put him down on the floor, still holding his collar.

And Remy rolled his eyes, took his T-shirt off while grappling with the collar, trading which hand was holding Hank as he removed the article of clothing.

Then, jeans and everything, he stepped into the tub, hanging on to Hank.

"Okay," he said to Lydia. "You're going to have to bathe both of us."

Lydia was standing there with water droplets on her shirt, and only then did he realize that the water had made her shirt transparent.

He could see the outline of her white bra, and that shouldn't mean a damn thing. It was a sedate enough one, and anyway, he'd seen so many women naked that something like this shouldn't register as necessarily erotic. Especially given that she was his best friend's little sister whom he had known most of his life.

And yet.

She was there; he was in the water. There was a giant dog between them, and the whole room began to smell like wet beast, and still . . .

"Sure," she said, meeting his gaze and lowering herself defiantly beside the tub.

She took his shampoo and conditioner combo off the side of the tub and began to lather up the dog, her hands coming dangerously close to his body.

What the hell kind of fever dream was this?

He wasn't impressed. Not with her, not with himself, not with the dog.

This felt like a bad setup for an erotic movie. And . . .

No. This was Lydia. Sweet Lydia that he had known forever. Sweet Lydia whose family meant the world to him.

And anyway, there was no way she was having sexual thoughts about him. Because she was . . . Then her eyes met his. And he felt genuine concern. Because there was nothing neutral about the way she was looking at him. She was looking at him as if . . . as if she definitely felt more than he would like.

But how was that possible? She was . . .

It was as if he could see a slideshow of their life, their connection. Of living in her parents' house, and seeing her at the breakfast table, smiling and laughing. Pretty, even at sixteen. Back when he'd also been a kid, and he had been . . .

Well, he'd been oblivious to her in that way.

For the first time, he had been living in a house that was filled with love, and he had been focused on that. On healing.

Like Hank. And in many ways, the Clay family had been the shelter he'd been sent to. He had been given cheese. And taught to trust. Even if just a little bit. And it had never even occurred to him to look at Lydia that way when . . .

Even now it felt like a sin.

And the worst part was, he was afraid that she wasn't opposed to mutual sinning.

Nope. He was putting that idea out of his head forever. She was Lydia. She was special. That was that.

# Chapter 6

Lydia's mouth was dry. She was glad there was nothing to talk about, because she wouldn't have been able to speak, even if she wanted to. The way Remy had looked at her . . . Well, also, the way Remy looked. Shirtless with water dripping down his muscular chest, holding the dog as if he was a precious baby . . . It was too much.

She genuinely couldn't cope.

Every time her hands skimmed over Hank's back, she came dangerously close to touching Remy's chest. The idea filled her with fear and longing, and she genuinely hated the intensity of both.

Because why was it like this, and why was she? Why did she have this . . . thing for him that she couldn't get rid of?

He was so comfortable with her that he had taken his clothes off and gotten into a bath. That was how little her presence meant to him. While he . . .

He was wrecking her.

This moment was wrecking her.

The dog was also full of lather, and she needed to do something, but she also wanted the moment to just end. So she did something without thinking. She stood up and turned the shower on. Hank leapt off Remy's lap and turned circles in the tub as if he was excited and definitely not afraid. Remy howled as cold water buffeted his chest and half drowned him where he sat.

But the dog was rinsed.

"Sorry!"

"You brat," he said, clearly not understanding that she had acted out of a sense of desperation rather than because she was trying to be an annoying younger sister.

But she didn't have time to say that, because he stood up, Hank leapt out of the tub, and then Remy pulled her in. Holding her fast, facing the showerhead so that she got drenched, his strong hands gripping her upper arms, heat and desire and freezing cold overtaking her all at once. It was erotic, confusing, and just far, far too much.

"If you can dish it out," he growled in her ear, "then you better be sure you can take it."

His words should've been a challenge. They should've made her angry. Instead, they made her ache with erotic longing.

She tried to pull away from him and then he ended up gripping her, turning her toward him, and their eyes met.

Just then, his eyes went wide, as if he realized what was happening.

Oh, dear. Remy could see it. He could see her. The way she felt about him. She felt small, and she felt upset. It wasn't fair. To be so plagued by this man. To not know what to do in this moment, because the truth was she didn't have any experience with men. No one could hold a candle to him, so she had just gone flameless instead.

She didn't know how to be flippant, how to play off a moment of sexual tension.

She didn't know how to live in it. How to defuse it, or how to progress it.

She felt stupid. Because he could see that she wanted him. And he was probably horrified, because why wouldn't he be?

Of course.

He had been treating her like a child. Yet to her, this felt erotic.

"Oh no," he said.

He turned and looked, and her gaze followed his, just in time to see Hank begin to shake, sending water flying all over the bathroom. All the way up to the ceiling.

And then Hank ran happily out of the room.

"Oh, shit," he said.

"Well. That's going to be . . . a mess."

He released his hold on her, and she got out of the bath.

"I'm soaking wet," she said.

Their eyes met, and the slow dawning realization of the double entendre embedded in those words filled her with a sense of horror.

"I mean . . . from the shower."

The fact that she felt the need to clarify didn't make it any better.

"Yeah. Anyway. I've got some clothes you can borrow."

"No. I should just go home."

"You're not driving home soaking wet like that. You'll get your car all wet, and you'll be uncomfortable. I'm sorry. You meant well, helping me with the dog. But . . . I just shouldn't have . . . I shouldn't have."

He turned the water off and got out of the bath, then walked down the hall, leaving wet footprints in his wake. She followed him slowly, hanging back. Then he opened up the drawers in his dresser, pulled out a pair of sweats and a T-shirt, and threw them in her direction. "You can change. I'll change. I'm just . . . Sorry about that."

He walked out of the bedroom, still wet, and left her standing there, holding the clothes.

She closed the door and began to peel the wet fabric away from her body. And ever so slowly, her mortification began to turn into anger.

Because Remy wasn't treating her like a woman. He was treating her like a child. She wasn't a child. She was a woman who'd had feelings for him for years and years. It was insulting that he had done that. That he had . . . grabbed her and pulled her into the bath like that.

And that he thought nothing of it. Nothing at all.

When she emerged from the bedroom she was warm and cozy but swimming in his clothes, and she felt completely lowered. Because the sweatpants, with their elastic bands at the ankles, made her feel like a toddler in a bunting, and that was not helping her mood.

"Do you want to stay for dinner?" he asked, standing in the door of his kitchen. The invitation made her feel suspicious. What she wanted to do was leave.

But it wasn't really a strange thing for him to ask. They shared meals at her parents' house all the time, and occasionally she ate over here with Matthew. But never by herself. Still, they were practically family.

It was just that she had always had trouble thinking of him that way.

Right now she was just so busy fulminating, she had no idea what she thought about anything.

But Hank was still pacing around, sodden, and she wanted . . . at the moment she couldn't tell whether she wanted to get past this feeling she was having or burn something to the ground.

One thing she knew: If she went home, nothing would be different. It would all be the same.

And she wasn't sure she could stomach that either.

"Sure," she said. "I would thank you for letting me use the clothes, but I'm not very grateful. On account of the fact that you're the one who got my other clothes wet."

She was holding them, a damp bundle in her arms.

"I'll put them in the dryer."

He took the clothes from her hands, including her underwear, and that made her feel warm, and yet even more spiteful. Because she was thinking about the intimacy of his seeing her bra and panties, but he most definitely wasn't.

She walked into the living room and sat down, petting Hank's wet head.

He appeared, arms crossed over his broad chest. "Hamburgers?"

"Of course. What's not to like about hamburgers?"

He shrugged.

Hank jumped up onto the couch, and she felt secretly pleased that he was going to leave a wet spot that was going to annoy Remy.

She was team "annoy Remy" just at the moment.

He walked back into the kitchen and she stayed on the couch for a while, patting Hank until she couldn't stand just listening to Remy move around anymore.

She got up and walked to the door of the kitchen, leaning there.

Remy walked to his stove, which had a big flat cast-iron grill over the top of two burners, and turned the heat on. Then he went over to the fridge and took out a couple of preprepared hamburger patties.

"Those are nice looking burgers," she offered, just to have something to say.

"I do appreciate that, for all you're a big lover of animals, you don't seem to be against my profession."

She was feeling sort of against him in a lot of ways right now, but not because he was a rancher. "I respect people who care for their animals, even when those animals are part of the food chain. I grew up country enough to understand the difference between what somebody like you does versus a factory farm. And I personally don't have the fortitude to be a vegetarian."

"Well, fair enough."

He put the meat on the grill, and the sizzling sound made her stomach growl even more fiercely.

She heard the sound of Hank's tags jingling as he slunk into the room looking baleful, as if Remy had betrayed him by cooking food not intended for him.

"Oh," he said. "I guess I should throw a third hamburger on."

"Are you really going to feed the dog hamburger?"

"Unless the pet police tells me that I can't." He opened up the fridge and grabbed a third patty.

"You just keep those in there?"

He laughed. "Beef is kind of my thing."

"Right."

"And the dog should have something nice."

She put aside all the confused feelings she had for him and wondered why she didn't think she deserved anything nice. Or rather, why she didn't push for more in her life.

Why she let him see her as the little sister, and why she'd always sort of accepted her lot in this town as being the weird girl who was either conspicuous when she didn't want to be, or cloaked in invisibility when she wished someone would notice her.

She'd thrown herself into taking care of animals, because they didn't think she was weird. Because they appreciated her, and so, too, did other animal people.

In her experience, animal people were often seen as weirdos. But to her, they were the good ones. The real ones. The ones who took time out to care for creatures that couldn't care for themselves. Possibly because of the ways in which people judged them and left them behind.

She couldn't resent her oddness because it had brought her to her passion, but she did resent . . .

That things sometimes still felt like high school.

This whole experience with Remy felt as if it had cemented something that she hadn't quite put a finger on before. She was *waiting*, and she had to stop.

She hadn't even realized it, but it was true.

No other man was Remy, so she'd never even tried to have a romantic relationship. Because one man saw her as a little sister, she'd sort of assumed this sexless identity that she just wasn't happy with anymore.

Irritation turned to determination.

She leaned against the door frame and looked at him, the strong set of his shoulders, the way he confidently cooked the burgers, then added slices of cheese.

"Have you . . . have you ever . . ." She trailed off. She was skirting close to dangerous territory right now. Bringing all this up. But part of her wanted to demystify him.

"What?"

"Have you ever had a girlfriend?"

He looked up from the grill and stared at her.

"No," he said. "Why?"

"Just curious."

"You ought to know."

"Well, you went away to college, and I don't know every-thing you did while you were there." She did *not* say *thank God*, but she thought it.

"No. I don't do the girlfriend thing. Like I said, I don't see my future including a long-term romantic relationship. It sounds like work. And I . . . Like I said, I love your family. They've been very good to me. But when I think about family, the Clays aren't the first people I think of. I think about being a kid and being shuttled back and forth between my mom and my dad, neither of whom really wanted me. It was kind of the opposite of a healthy custody exchange. My mom didn't run to hug me and welcome me home. It was more like: *You again.* I put a damper on her social life. And as far as my dad . . . If he liked having me with him at all, it was because it gave him someone to bully. That's not better."

Her heart went tight. "No."

"I would never put a kid through that."

"But you're not your parents."

"That's the question I have, Lydia. What makes you into a person like them?"

She didn't have it in her to be irritated at him now. Because this wasn't about her crush, her issues, the things she projected onto him.

"Do you think that your dad would ever have taken in a dog like Hank, let him sleep on the couch, then fried him up a hamburger?"

"I guess not."

"Do you think your mom would ever add to her workload by offering to take care of three extra horses that she didn't even need?"

"Well . . . no."

"And do you think that either of them would've had the discipline you did in school? To take advantage of all the opportunities you had. Do you think they would've planned their future meticulously the way you did, invested their time and energy into the sorts of pursuits you took up?"

"The ability to make money has nothing to do with character."

"Maybe not. I'm sure there are dirt-poor animal rescuers. But what it does show is that you have the ability to think about something other than what satisfies you right that very moment. I think both of your parents can be characterized by their inability to care at all what anyone else wanted from them or needed from them. I think they essentially just cared about their own feelings, and no one else's. And there are so many things you do that demonstrate you're not that person."

"Appreciated, moppet."

He made it hard. To not love him. To stay mad.

He assembled the burgers, and they sat down at the table. He put the patty he'd cooked up for Hank in a bowl, and the dog settled down beside Remy's chair.

His use of her childhood nickname made her uncomfortable. A combination of prickly and a little bit . . . Oh, she didn't want to be aroused. It was because they were in his house, because they were alone.

She didn't think any of this conversation was going to make him see her differently. But she wanted to shake something up. To shake him up, or maybe just her.

"Well . . . I . . . I'd like to get married someday." She picked her burger up and took a bite.

"Sure you do. You had a great family. You would be a great mom. I can tell by the way you take care of all those animals. Though I suppose if you only want to have furry children, that would work just as well."

"I would take both," she said, her chest feeling sore. She was young to be thinking about children, she knew, but not too young to want to start taking the steps to get there.

"Well, I've never had a boyfriend."

He looked at her, regarding her closely. "Is that right?"

"Yes. And you know, it's a real problem, being a virgin at twenty-seven. Because how are you supposed to ever make anything happen? At that point, you're just weird."

He froze. "What the hell are you talking about?"

"Just what I said." She felt foolish for confessing, but he'd talked about his own reputation, and picking up partners with her brother along.

"Actually, if there's one problem I really feel like I need to solve right now, my virginity is the one."

She hadn't *meant* to say that. She really, really hadn't.

Except . . . she had been feeling this frustration. Desperation. A need to make him . . . see her differently.

*Yeah, and him knowing you're a latter-day virgin is really going to lift that veil. Really going to make you seem cool and edgy and sexy . . .*

She focused on her burger. "I'm sorry," she said. "I didn't mean to throw that at you. I . . . things just come out of my mouth sometimes and . . ." She took another bite of her burger. "This is great," she said, talking around the mouthful.

He was just looking at her and not saying anything.

"Are you . . . do you have someone in mind?" he asked, finally, sounding as if he had a piece of hamburger lodged in his throat.

*You.*

She didn't say that. "Not . . . no." She finished her hamburger faster than any other human had ever finished one and slid out of her chair. "I need to go. I just realized it's late and I have an early start tomorrow. Well, every day because animals don't sleep in just because you want them to!"

She smiled and pushed her chair in.

He looked a little confused but didn't stop her. "Okay. See you later."

"Yeah. See you."

When she got out to her car, she sat in the driver's seat and pressed her forehead to the steering wheel for two solid minutes, replaying the stupidity of what she'd just said.

But by the time she got home, she'd started rationalizing, and when she tucked herself into bed she was almost calm.

Because she'd known Remington Lane for most of her life, and one cringeworthy moment wasn't going to expose her entirely to him. That confession was something she could almost tell her brother (she wouldn't, but she could see a scenario where it could have come up and she might have) and Remy was . . . like a brother.

In his mind.

He didn't know she thought of him the way she did.

And he never had to.

She hadn't exposed herself. She hadn't changed anything at all.

Remy was focused on Hank. As he should be.

She repeated that mantra in her head until she fell asleep.

# Chapter 7

The trouble was, Remy couldn't get what she'd said out of his head.

But it mingled with the images of her, wet and in his arms, in the shower. What a foolish, idiotic, stupid move he'd made, pulling her in and . . .

She was a virgin.

He'd seen her bra.

He'd felt her shape pressed all up against him when he'd . . .

God Almighty.

He was trying. He had plenty to do. Animals to feed, and he was working on a new game, which gave him a packed schedule for pretty much every hour of the day that he was awake.

But he kept replaying it, over and over again.

*I need to lose my virginity.*

The truth was, he had never given much thought to what all Lydia got up to in her spare time. Romantically.

She was Lydia Clay. She was an enigma. A special sort of creature who seemed to exist outside and above the base sorts of nonsense that other human beings got up to. At least, that was how he had always chosen to see her.

The truth was, she was beautiful. He had known that for years.

But he thought of her as something like a fairy. Not a woman you could actually reach out and touch. God, no.

He didn't think of her that way.

*Oh no? How about when you just suddenly realized that she was a woman?*

*How about when you gave Hank a bath and got a good look at her figure and chose to touch her like the asshole you are?*

He'd been messing with her. That was all. Like she was a sister . . .

*Liar. You wanted to touch her.*

He winced and shoved that thought to the side. He didn't need to go having thoughts like that. But then he'd asked that question about who she wanted to lose her virginity with.

She said she didn't have anyone in mind. But he wondered.

Yeah. He did wonder.

And because he was marinating on the issue with Lydia, he was uncertain how he felt when Matthew called and invited him to dinner at his parents' place.

Eating at the Clays' was a regular thing. It wasn't formal or anything, and often the invites came last minute. But he ended up having dinner there once a month at a minimum. Tom Clay would barbecue, while Nancy Clay would make macaroni and cheese and dinner rolls that were to die for, and typically a cream pie of some kind.

The kind of domestic bliss that had been completely foreign to Remy when he was a child. He had been convinced, actually, that the happy family was all a lie made up by media. Until he had started spending time with this family. Whose members clearly loved each other, and actually took part in these sorts of rituals. Family dinners, quality time.

They didn't just do it, they did it joyfully.

They continued to do it, even with their children well into adulthood. They continued to invite him, as if he was actually part of the family, and not only because he was a sad child they felt sorry for.

That was the thing.

They didn't need to include him in their get-togethers. They just did.

And it was an amazing thing.

So even with inappropriate thoughts about touching Lydia pinging around in his brain, he said yes to the dinner invitation.

Nancy texted him and asked him to bring his new dog.

Of course, the Clay household was animal friendly.

So that was how he and Hank found themselves loading up in the truck on Sunday night for family dinner. His stomach growled.

He had great food at home. But there was just something about a home-cooked meal from . . .

Nancy wasn't his mom. But the truth was, she was the closest thing he had. And it was special to have her cook for him. It reminded him of when he was fifteen, completely blown away that an adult might care about him to the degree that she seemed to. His own parents couldn't seem to be bothered.

The past had seemed so much closer the last few weeks. Ever since his dad had died.

He wasn't sad. There was nothing to be sad about. His father was a prick. The end.

But death sure made a man go over old ground he thought he'd long ago left behind.

His confused thoughts made him ache when he drove up to the Clay house. When he saw the porch light on, that porch light that had always been on for him even though it didn't have to be.

He scowled, parked his truck and got out, taking the time to go to the passenger seat and lift Hank out gently.

He never wanted to make the old dog jump out on his own.

It didn't seem right.

Hank followed him right up to the front door, and Nancy opened it before he could knock.

"Come in, come in," she said, pulling him in for a hug before pushing him into the house.

Her love was aggressive. And appreciated.

Then she stepped away from him and looked down at Hank. "And who is this distinguished gentleman?"

"This is Hank," he said.

She looked up at him. "Lydia said that he belonged to your dad."

"Yeah," he said, his voice rough for some reason now.

"How are you doing with that, Remy?"

"Just fine. He didn't have any impact on my life."

She looked at him as if she felt sadness, but not pity.

She rubbed his shoulder. "Well. If you ever need to talk, you know you can talk to me."

He nodded.

When he stepped deeper into the house, he could smell the aromas of all his favorites. "Thanks for having me over."

"Of course. It's not a family dinner if you're not here."

He believed her. That was the amazing thing. He really did believe it.

"Matthew and Jackson are on their way. They said it took forever to get Wesley into the car."

He chuckled. "Better them than me."

"You would be a wonderful father," she said.

The words hit him oddly. "Well, that's a nice thing to . . . to say. But I can't actually imagine . . ."

Right then, Lydia came down the stairs, wearing a floaty white dress, the kind of thing he rarely saw her in, because she was usually dressed for the shelter or to take care of her animals.

She stopped and looked at him, her cheeks going pink, and everything in him went quiet.

That moment back at his place replayed in his head. And he had to wonder . . .

What would have happened if he'd kissed her then?

If he'd pressed her against the wall of the shower and . . .

For God's sake. He had to get his head on straight.

"It fits," she said, her cheeks getting even pinker.

"So it does," said Nancy. "I won't get rid of it then."

"What's this?" he asked.

"Oh, Mom wanted me to try on a couple of her old dresses."

"Looks good," he said.

The moment stretched between them, and it was as if no one else was there. He hadn't meant to pay her the compliment, and yet, it was true, and she more than deserved it. Because she looked absolutely beautiful. Her blond hair was down around her shoulders, and the delicate fabric conformed to her figure beautifully.

Historically, he hadn't spent a lot of time thinking about Lydia's figure. Lately, though, it was on his mind a lot.

*And no one has ever touched her.*

That thought came straight from hell. And he rebuked it and sent it right back.

"Thank you," she said, the word coming out slightly breathless.

"Wear it for dinner," her mom said, looking between the two of them.

He straightened as if he had been called out by a drill sergeant.

"Oh, I might get something on it."

"I was going to throw it away, so there's no use hoarding it and never wearing it because you might get it dirty."

Nancy smiled at him and then turned to walk into the

kitchen. Leaving him and Lydia by themselves in the living room.

"I never wear dresses," she said. "It feels a little bit silly."

"It doesn't look silly."

She was a virgin.

She wanted to change that.

She was dressed, at this moment, slightly like a virgin sacrifice.

Hank began to whine, and then the front door opened again, and they were saved by the arrival of Matthew, Jackson and baby Wesley, who was perched on Matthew's hip wearing a dinosaur costume. Lydia's face lit up as she crossed in front of him, straight to the entry, where she plucked Wesley from her brother's arms. "There's my favorite nephew in the whole world."

"Your only nephew in the whole world," Matthew pointed out.

"Don't get too technical, because then that makes your being my favorite brother null and void. And also Jackson's being my favorite brother-in-law."

Remy stepped forward and took Matthew's hand, brought him in for a brief hug, clapped him on the back twice, then did the same with Jackson.

Lydia took Wesley and twirled with him into the kitchen, growling like a dinosaur. Remy looked down at Hank. "I don't actually have a clue how Hank is around little kids."

Matthew smiled. "I doubt that Wesley is in any danger of being put down here. Between my sister and Grandma and Grandpa, that kid may actually never learn to walk."

They all filtered into the kitchen, Hank cautiously sniffing the newcomers. He walked over to Lydia and lifted his nose, sniffing around Wesley's foot.

He doubted the poor old dog had ever been included in a

family gathering. And he had never related to an animal more—sniffing around this warm, civilized house, that was so unlike anywhere he had ever been before.

Yeah, he related to that hard.

Tom came into the house carrying a tray stacked with ribs, and Lydia recoiled. "Mom," she said. "You didn't say Dad was serving ribs when you told me to keep the white dress on."

"I'll get you a lobster bib," she said.

"Mom!"

But Nancy was already at the drawer, pulling out one of those plastic bibs that actually had a lobster on it, and Lydia looked horrified.

"And you can put one in your lap too."

Her dad set the ribs down in the center of the table, and then took Wesley from her while her mom accosted her with bibs.

"Once the baby of the family, always the baby of the family," Matthew said. "Even when there's a literal baby."

Lydia looked flat as she sat down at the table, but once all the food was laid out in front of her, she couldn't look grumpy anymore. And her frown gave him something to focus on other than how pretty she looked, even with the lobster bib.

Corn on the cob, macaroni and cheese, ribs, dinner rolls, coleslaw and a key lime pie as well as a coconut cream pie. This was home. This was family.

*So why do you think you don't know what family is?*

Maybe his attitude was a poor tribute to this family that had given him so much. Maybe.

But there was a division between him and them. And he honestly didn't know if a few years of being part of this clan could erase the heritage of his actual blood.

If he could bring himself to care even a little bit more about his dad, then he might feel sorry that the old man had gone to the grave without ever knowing the joy of real family. Without ever understanding it. Remy might feel slightly outside the circle, but at least he knew it was real.

At least he knew it could be.

Lydia picked up her rib and began to nibble at it delicately. Then she put one finger in her mouth and licked barbecue sauce away, then her thumb.

She was a virgin.

That knowledge echoed inside him as he watched the way her tongue moved over her own skin.

What the hell was wrong with him?

She shouldn't have told him she was a virgin. That was the bottom line.

He looked down, forcing himself to focus on his food.

There was conversation going on around him, but it was difficult for him to track. He looked down at Hank, who was staring at him balefully. And he gave the dog some meat off his rib.

"No feeding dogs at the table," said Nancy, as if he was fourteen years old, but part of him appreciated the rule.

"Poor Hank has been through a lot," said Lydia.

And again, he sort of felt that they could be talking about him.

"It's true," Remy said. "He has. I'm trying to make up for it."

When it was time to serve pie, Lydia got up to make coffee, and he couldn't help but take notice of her long legs, showcased to perfection by the short white dress.

She really should wear dresses more often.

"Success," Matthew said. "You're barbecue sauce free, Lydia."

She gave her brother a thumbs-up, and treated him to an irritated facial expression, but then brought the pot of coffee, along with mugs, back to the table.

Remy decided to assist with serving pie, and then after he had laid out plates for everybody, took one piece of each for himself.

Lydia did the same and started sipping her coffee.

He had just about shoveled the last bite of pie into his mouth when Lydia made an outraged noise. "Oh, of course," she said. "I spilled coffee on this like I have a hole in my lip."

"We'll just clean it right away," her mom said.

"Okay."

"I am cleaning out the upstairs," Nancy said, turning her attention to him. "So you should run up and check out the boxes in your old room."

"I already came by and did mine," Matthew said. "Not that any of you care. Maybe Mom just threw all my things away."

"Sure, golden boy," he said. "That's likely."

Lydia got up from her chair and went over to the sink, getting a washcloth wet, and dabbing at the front of her dress. He decided to take that as his cue to go upstairs.

"I'll just go check it out."

He hadn't been upstairs in the house in some time. Maybe not since he'd moved out. There just wasn't really a reason to. There was a guest bathroom downstairs, and sometimes he felt reluctant to take a walk down memory lane. Yes, he had childhood memories here, but . . . it was all complicated.

This had been the best time of his life in many ways. But being here also made him ache. He pushed open the door that led to his teenage bedroom. He had had his own bedroom here. It still blew his mind. That they had been so generous to him.

The space looked different now. No posters on the wall.

And a few boxes in the center of the room. He opened one up and looked inside.

His yearbook.

Yes. It was past time he took the stuff with him.

It really said a lot that he was going through things at this house at the same time as Matthew and Lydia.

That maybe, just maybe, this was his family. And he did belong.

Yeah, because family would be checking out Lydia's legs.

There was an outdated PlayStation, but he was actually feeling nostalgic, so he figured he would keep it. And there was a birthday card in the box with puppies on the front. He frowned. But he opened it up and saw that it was from Lydia. For his seventeenth birthday.

Of course she had given him a card with puppies. Even if it wasn't his thing, it was very much hers. And she wouldn't be able to imagine anything more charming. He chuckled.

It was just so . . . her.

Sweet. And a little bit lost in her own world. But he liked that about her. He always had.

The door creaked, and he looked up. And there she was, standing there in that white dress, looking at him.

"Yes?"

"I just . . . I was curious what was . . ."

"A birthday card from you."

She slipped inside. "Really?"

"Yes. You hoped that my birthday was *paws-itively* wonderful." He handed her the card as she crouched down by the box, moving to her knees. She looked at the card and laughed. "What was I thinking?"

"The same thing you were thinking when you brought me a damned dog. You can't imagine anybody not finding this as charming as you do."

"Well, that makes me sound selfish."

"You're not selfish."

He looked at her profile, at the way her blond hair fell into her face. She was sweet in ways that no one else he knew was. She was the last person on earth who could ever be considered selfish. She just cared *so much* about the things she cared about, she couldn't understand that other people might not. He knew that intuitively. Understood it.

"What else is in the box? Or is it personal?"

He didn't know what possessed him then. "Industrial-sized bottle of lube and a giant box of condoms."

She looked up at him, the card open in her hands, her eyes round.

"I'm kidding," he said.

"Well. Well . . . I mean, I am quite certain that . . . in high school . . ."

"I wasn't getting up to anything in high school. Not here. Can you imagine? Me being my father's son, I would've been chased out of girls' bedrooms with a shotgun."

"Oh. Well. I mean, I assumed that . . ."

"Did you make assumptions about me?"

He was inching way too close to the thing that had been haunting him these last several days.

"I wondered. Of course I did. I am the lame younger sister. Of course I always wondered what you and Matthew were doing. You were so much cooler than me."

"Well, for obvious reasons, neither Matthew nor I really came online until we left here. But we were very cool in college." He and Matthew had actually been roommates at the University of Oregon, which they'd decided to attend together.

"I guess so. And as the younger sister, I guess I never thought the logistics through. I just thought you were both cool."

He chuckled. "Well, I was from the wrong side of the tracks, and Matthew . . . you know. Once we got to college we cut loose. It wasn't so easy in a town full of people who all thought they knew us."

"Right."

"Is that your problem?"

*Don't ask about that, you idiot.*

She blinked. "My problem?"

"Yeah. You said that you . . ."

"Oh, I remember what I said. Thank you. But no. I'm not

gay, and I'm not from the wrong side of the tracks, as I think you know."

"That isn't what I meant. What I meant is when you live somewhere all your life, people have an expectation about who you are. Which is really what I was up against too. Folks think they know you. And because of that, they think they know what you want, or at least what you ought to want."

"Oh. Well. I've always been weird. I've always been the girl with cages of animals in her room, the one you could bring a sick bird to. But yeah, guys are reluctant to date that girl."

"Not now, though."

"It would take a very particular kind of man to sign on for all this."

It was true in some ways, but in others, her comment irked him. The idea that somehow men wouldn't see she was a great girl. Sweet and caring.

"Then what is it?"

"Well. I'm twenty-seven. After a certain point, it gets weird. In college I felt like an outsider. When I came home, I hadn't met anyone yet. Then I just still didn't. You are right about the hometown thing being weird in some respects. You can't really casually hook up with somebody unless . . . I don't know. Unless you really think about it. Unless you know what you're doing. I didn't know what I was doing. Or even what I wanted."

"So at this point, some of the problem is the barrier of having never done it."

She snorted. "Done it. This does remind me of high school." She looked up at him, and suddenly her blue eyes were grave. "Remy . . . if you . . . I . . ."

She didn't ask. She didn't verbalize what he thought she might. But his heart stopped all the same, his stomach went tight. Here they were, sitting on the bedroom floor that he'd once called his own. He had lived here, and so had she. Her parents had been very trusting to allow that. To let him live in the same house as their teenage daughter. God knew he would never, ever have done anything untoward then.

He was thinking about it now. But then, she was twenty-seven.

As she had just reminded him.

"Lydia . . ."

"If you don't . . ." She looked so wounded, she couldn't even finish the sentence. And that did it.

Because suddenly the words that had been echoing inside his head roared through him like a freight train, and he realized he did want to do something about them.

He couldn't leave her looking like that. He reached out and cupped her face, holding her steady as he leaned in and kissed her.

She drew in a breath as soon as their mouths touched, and the sweet sigh nearly undid him.

Remington Lane had kissed any number of women, but none of them had ever been like this.

There wasn't any knowing involved before. And he knew Lydia Clay.

He knew her better than he knew just about anyone. He knew the way she sighed, and the way she laughed. He knew the way she cared for others, whether they be human or animal. He knew the way she lit up when she saw her nephew, and how she loved her family. Most of all, he knew the way she looked in this white dress, and how it had set his blood on fire from the moment he'd walked through the front door tonight, even if he hadn't wanted to admit that's what it was.

The connection between them was made up of so many moments.

Going back before she had brought him Hank, but it had certainly intensified recently.

And he was obsessed with the fact that no man had ever touched her before.

Obsessed to the point of madness.

So now he was kissing her. Not just a test. Not only a taste.

He angled his head and took the kiss deeper. She parted her lips, responding, the tip of her tongue testing the tip of his.

He groaned, unable to believe that he was doing this here.

But more able to believe he was doing it with her than he would have ever imagined.

He moved away from her and studied her face.

Her pupils were dilated, her eyes wide, her lips parted just slightly. "That's what I was trying to ask for," she said. "For a start."

"You want me to take your virginity." Just saying it made his stomach knot up hard. Made him feel . . .

He was turned on. Hell.

He hadn't imagined any of the moments between them. Not at her place, not during Hank's bath. Not when she'd looked him dead in the eye and told him she'd never been with anyone before.

It was about him. About the two of them, and hell and damn if that didn't . . .

Thrill him.

Was it a completely messed up thing to want to be a woman's first? He had never really considered that before. It had never mattered. It just mattered because it was her. If it wasn't him, then it was going to be somebody. Lydia was sweet, and she was pure. She was untouched by so many of the things in this world. She had had a good childhood, a sweet one. She hadn't had to deal with any of the things that he'd had to deal with as a kid. It was why she always seemed more fay than human to him. Almost otherworldly.

And it was completely fair that she wanted to have . . . more. Everything. She should have it. Maybe it was selfish, twisting up the truth to think that it was a good thing for him to introduce her to sex. But he would make it good. Hell, he would make it great. He was very, very in tune with women's bodies. He was fascinated by how things worked, after all. The study of the female orgasm was one that he had dedicated himself to and took very seriously.

Hell, when a man engaged in casual sex, he had to be an expert on body language. He had to be good at communicating and extracting communication from the other person.

He made it his mission.

He would do right by her.

Somewhere in the back of his mind, he chastised himself. For twisting this up, for creating a scenario where somehow he was a saint for getting to have sex.

Except, it could never be that basic, not with Lydia.

Because she was special. That was all he knew.

"Yes," she said slowly. "But . . . only if you want me. Because you've known me a very long time, and you've never seemed the least bit interested, and then I went and opened my big mouth the other day at the table, and now I have basically made myself as pathetic as possible and begged you. . . ."

"You didn't beg," he said. "You sent signals, and I responded to them. I'm a pretty hardheaded man, Lydia. And it has suited me to think of you as my best friend's much younger sister for a very long time. But you're a woman. You're not a girl. Regardless of how I've liked to think of you."

"When did that change?"

"I can't really say when. There have been shifts over time. I started really noticing how beautiful you are . . . as a woman, recently."

"Is that the same as wanting?"

Right then, in this house, sitting so close to her, it felt the same as breathing. Essential. He couldn't remember not wanting her—that was the strangest part of this conversation. He couldn't remember what it was like to want anyone else.

"I can't stand the thought of another man touching you. Not first. Haven't I been there for you?"

"Yes."

"Going to be there for you this way too. If you want it."

"I want," she said. "Have I said anything that's been ambiguous? It's you that I'm worried about. I don't want pity sex. I don't want you to have sex with me because I am Matthew's weird little sister and—"

He silenced her with a kiss. He silenced her with all the passion pent up inside him, and what really terrified him in that moment was how right it felt. Because it was one thing to be aroused, and it was quite another to feel replete, with a sense that he was home. The same sort of feeling he'd gotten when he'd pulled up to the house today and seen the porch light on, when he had come up to this room, that was the feeling that flooded him now. With her mouth on his.

Home.

Safe and precarious all at once. Wonderful and aching.

"Are you still questioning me?"

She shook her head, her eyes wide.

"So, your mission, should you choose to accept it, is to try and go back downstairs without looking like we've been making out." Because this was the danger. He loved the Clay family more than anything, and he would never have sex with Lydia simply because he wanted a woman, but he knew how the hell it would seem to her family.

They wouldn't understand this feeling.

This feeling of . . . responsibility that he felt for her pleasure, for her happiness.

And hell, he wouldn't want to get into it with any of them. Because this was between Lydia and him. This was theirs.

Sacred in that way.

"I can do that," she said, her voice trembling.

"I'll bring down my box of stuff."

"I was supposed to change."

"No. Keep that dress on."

Because he was going to take it off later.

If that made him a terrible person, then he supposed he was just going to have to accept going to hell.

Because tonight he was going to take Lydia Clay to heaven.

Of that he was certain.

# Chapter 8

He had kissed her. She did her very best to go back downstairs and not look as if he had just kissed her. Her head was spinning.

Somehow, she had gone from being absolutely certain that Remington Lane would never see her as anything more than a child, to being embarrassed about what she had said about her virginity, to being . . . very nearly grateful for it.

Because he was going to . . .

It was what she wanted. She wanted him to be the first.

She wanted him to be the only, that was the problem. She had feelings for him that were so much deeper than she would like, but maybe this was the only way to get past them.

Maybe this was the only way to pursue being a normal woman. One who could look at other men and want them.

Maybe she had to mark this occasion. Maybe she had to answer the question—what would it be like to have Remy?

If nothing else, whether it fixed something or broke it more, she was about to live out a fantasy. And very few people could ever claim to live out their fantasies.

Up until now, she never had.

Mostly, her fantasies stayed locked in a box that she couldn't access. Mostly, they were nothing she could reach.

But she could reach him now.

She swallowed hard, her throat feeling scratchy.

"I thought you were going to change," her mom said, as Lydia's foot hit the last step.

"Oh. I . . . I'm going to wash the dress when I get home."

"All right. Cold water."

"Yeah. Thanks, Mom."

"I know. You don't need me to tell you what to do."

"Sometimes I do," she said.

Remy came down the stairs then, holding a box, and Lydia didn't think it was her imagination that her mom's gaze lingered on him for an extra moment. But she didn't say anything.

"I'll just go say goodbye to the boys."

Lydia slipped into the kitchen and gave Wesley a giant kiss on his chubby cheek, then said goodbye to Matthew and Jackson.

And her father.

Hank had been waiting patiently by the table. Probably hoping for more treats.

She reached down and petted him on the head. Somehow, she had a feeling he was responsible for all of this.

Whatever all this turned out to be.

"See you all," Remy said, sticking his head in. "Come on, Hank."

The dog stood up and was instantly glued right to Remy's heel.

She ducked out the front door, walking alongside the two of them. "Do you think it's obvious that we're leaving together so we can . . ."

"No. Because believe me, nobody would . . ."

Of course. Nobody would suspect what they were about to do. If Remy hadn't even seen her as a woman a week ago, why would anyone think they were about to get together?

Just because it all felt big and obvious and real to her.

She blinked and watched as he helped Hank up into his truck, her heart squeezing.

And then, once in the privacy of her own car, safely distant from her family, she started to tremble.

They were going to have sex.

She didn't know any other man the way she knew Remy. She knew him better than she knew almost anyone else. They had been part of each other's lives for years. She had literally lived with him.

She wanted him.

She fantasized about him. She burned for him.

She also realized she hadn't established where they were going. But before she could pick up her phone to call him, he called her.

"We are obviously going to my house. I am not having sex in the presence of a raccoon."

She laughed. Because honestly, that was the most ridiculous thing he had ever said. "My bedroom has a working door."

"Raccoons have hands."

"The door has a lock. Anyway, he can't reach the door-knob."

"What about if he put his hand under the door where I could see it and flexed his little raccoon fingers?"

Pascal had done that before. "I can't make any promises one way or the other."

"The sex is happening in my house."

"Well. Okay."

Neither of them said anything for a moment. "What do you think you like?" He asked that question all throaty and low. And it took her off guard.

"I don't know. I haven't had sex before, remember."

"Yeah, but you must have fantasized."

*About you, idiot.*

"Your kiss was better than any kiss I've ever had. I feel like I just . . . Go with that and you'll probably be pretty set."

"It's a good thought. But I want to know. Fast, slow. Rough?"

"All of the above?"

She was sweaty. Her heart was beating so fast she thought she might actually pass out.

She was grateful when they pulled up to his house and it was finally . . . time.

She put her car in park, turned off the engine and nearly tumbled right out.

But as soon as her shoe hit the gravel, she looked up and saw that he was there.

Like Prince Charming in a cowboy hat. He reached his hand out, and she took it. The gesture was so much more loaded than any other contact they'd ever had. It was different.

Her heart squeezed tight.

"Are you good?"

"Oh, I'm very good," she said.

"I want to make it clear to you that you're more to me than Matthew's little sister. I think the world of you. You know that, right?"

His words, so sincere, so deep, left her breathless. "I . . . I can't say I do know that. But it feels good to hear."

"You're one of the people who makes me believe in the good of this world. I think basically all of those people share your last name."

She huffed slightly. "Well, is it me or is it my family?"

"Let's put it this way—no one else in your family is here. It's you. So yes, your family may feel a certain way about people, about connection. But you're the only one who . . ."

She laughed. "In fairness, I'm the only one who would've been available to you, who would also be your type."

"It's not like that."

She let him lead her into the house. Hank followed them and immediately jumped up onto the couch, unperturbed by whatever they might be planning.

She knew that no matter what, she would never regret this. It wasn't possible. It was something that she had wanted for a very long time. Him.

"Kiss me."

So he did, right there in the entryway of his house, first with his hands spanning her waist, then moving up her back, before he wrapped his arms around her entirely and brought her in close as he consumed her.

It was far more intense than she had ever imagined a kiss could be. And if she had any insecurity about him not wanting her, about this not being what he really wanted, it was laid to rest nicely at the altar of that kiss.

She looked at him, and her whole body felt strung out on a wire. Pulled as tight as it could possibly go without snapping.

Because this was Remington Lane, a man she had known most of her life. A man she had cared for, over so many years. Looking both familiar and like a stranger all at once.

The very object of her fantasies and also an enigma she didn't think she had ever truly known until this moment. After all, did you really know a man when you didn't know what he tasted like? How he kissed?

How he made love.

The very idea made her shiver, shudder.

Maybe she didn't know what she was doing. But they had transformed this thing between them into something new, something magical, and she had been part of that. So maybe she wasn't as inept as she feared.

His hands moved over her body, and she arched against him, ready for everything, ready for him.

She had been, for years.

He pushed his hands up underneath her dress, his rough palms scraping against her skin. She gasped.

When he parted from her, he was breathing heavily, raggedly. She could see that he was on the edge of his control. There was barely any left, if there had ever been any at all.

She wrapped her arms around his neck, pushing her fingers through his hair and shivering.

He propelled them both down the hallway, to his bedroom. It was neat and immaculate, the same as the rest of the house.

The sight made her heart ache, just slightly.

He had made a beautiful facsimile of a home, but he didn't think that he deserved to have a family. He took such pains to exercise ruthless control over all of his surroundings. It was evident in every detail of this place.

But he had brought Hank in.

Yes, out of a sense of duty because of what his father had done, but also because he just cared. At the end of the day, Remington Lane was a good man. He always had been. And she had always known it. It was why she could trust him now with her body. Oh, how she wished that she could trust him with her heart.

Yes, she wished that.

But for now, she would just give him everything else, simply everything she had to offer.

She unbuttoned his shirt, revealing his muscles, and she trembled with desire.

He was so beautiful. Every hard-cut line of his body was now more than just a fantasy. He was reality. A beautiful fantasy made masculine flesh before her, and she could scarcely believe the gift of him.

She pressed her palm to the center of his chest, moved her fingertips over that rough hair and hot skin.

"Oh," she breathed.

"Lydia," he said. She looked up, her eyes meeting his. "You good?"

"I'm better than good," she said.

"Perfect."

And that was when she found herself stripped of that white dress. When she found herself standing nearly naked before him, only covered by her insubstantial white bra and cotton underwear. It was hardly the outfit she would've chosen for losing her virginity, had she planned ahead. But he didn't seem to mind at all. "I always knew that you were some special kind of beautiful. Like something from another world. The kind of sweet, the kind of generous that I didn't think existed. But I didn't guess. . . . You're a damned miracle, Lydia Clay."

His words were like balm for her soul. Like a magical gift. Because if weird Lydia Clay could be a miracle to Remington Lane, then maybe all her weirdness was okay after all. Maybe it was a gift.

He made her feel as if everything she'd ever done meant something in a way she hadn't been certain it did before.

Maybe she shouldn't need a few words of affirmation from the man who held her in his arms, but it was a beautiful thing that she had it.

She hadn't been waiting for it, not really.

She would never let it go now.

He lowered her slowly onto the bed, kissed her neck, down her collarbone, to the plump curve of her breast, the edge of her lace bra cup.

"Are you wet now, Lydia?" he growled, his lips against her skin.

She nearly flew off the mattress. "Yes," she whispered. "Not from the shower."

He growled against her skin, and her internal muscles clenched tight with need.

Sex as a fantasy was one thing. It was gauzy and sweet in her mind. It felt good, but in an impressionistic way. Out of focus dabs of pleasure coming together to create a half-imagined scene. This was not that.

It was sharp. In great, detailed focus. Every pinpoint of desire was fully realized. Drawn in exquisite detail.

The way his lips touched her skin, his tongue tracing shapes there.

The way his hands moved over her body, the weight of him as he settled over the top of her, the heat of his mouth.

She was so aware of the shift of fabric as he unhooked her bra. How rough his jeans were against her thighs. And all of it was good. Brilliant, wonderful.

He kissed a line straight to her nipple, sucked it deep into his mouth, the sound of satisfaction on his lips stoking the fires of desire deep within her.

Then he moved to her other breast, the attention he lavished upon her decadent, glorious. She had always considered herself a practical girl. This was not practical. It was not simply about maintenance. It was simply extra.

It was the joy and ecstasy of being human in a way that she had never quite experienced before. It was connection.

Was it the same for him?

She hoped it was. She wished it could be. So much. Down to the depths of her soul, that was what she wanted.

He kissed his way down her body to the waistband of her panties. He pulled them down, and she didn't even have time to be embarrassed. He dragged them away from her legs, cast them on the floor, and then he was kissing her, right at the tender part of her inner thigh.

And then higher still.

Right to the place where she was wet and aching for him. And then he devoured her. As if she was the most glorious feast he had ever set eyes on. It *was* glorious. She had never felt anything like this. She had never even imagined that pleasure like this was real.

She had thought it was the bastion of fake orgasms on late-night cable TV, and overly florid descriptions in the romance novels she had stolen from her mother's bedroom when she was a teen, only to discard them because they had hurt too much when she had realized what she wanted from Remy, and that she was unlikely to ever get it.

But now she knew. She knew. It wasn't fake. It was very, very real. White-hot pleasure scalded her. Her desire built and built until she shattered. Until she clung to his shoulders and cried out his name.

Then he moved up to kiss her on the lips, and she heard the drawer to his nightstand open.

She thanked God that he had the presence of mind to protect them both, because she certainly didn't.

She put her hands on his belt buckle, and undid it slowly. Then she helped him strip his jeans and underwear off. Until he was naked in front of her.

She just about lost her nerve then.

He was big and thick, gorgeous and glorious.

She had never seen a man quite like him. Of course, she had never seen a naked man before. Not in person.

She hadn't imagined that she would find one quite so beautiful. But Remy was perfect. He was everything. Everything she had ever dreamed of and then some.

Tears pricked her eyes, and she blinked them back. She didn't want to be emotional about this. It was difficult not to be.

She had gone from being so certain that this was something that would never happen, to living in the reality of it.

And finding out that he was better. More than she had ever hoped he could be.

He tore open the condom, and she watched as his large masculine hand guided it over his hard length.

Excitement coursed through her, along with just a little bit of fear.

But not enough that it was going to stop her from having this. From having him.

He kissed her, deep and long, put his hands between her thighs and stroked her until she was whimpering again.

"We'll take it slow," he said.

He pushed one finger inside her, then a second. He stretched her gently, and she arched against him, begging for more with a wordless plea.

She wanted him. All of him.

He withdrew from her, and then positioned himself between her legs, pressing the head of his arousal against the entrance to her body. He entered her slowly, inch by agonizing inch. And she gritted her teeth as he stretched her, as she took all of him.

She clung to his shoulders, dug her fingernails into his skin. It was perfect. It was wonderful.

It was everything.

And then, Remington Lane was inside her. Just as she had dreamed, but also more than she had ever dreamed. Because this was deeper, more profound than that impressionist painting in her mind. It was more than simple fantasy or sexual arousal. It was much more.

Better. Deeper.

But she did wonder if she had miscalculated. Because this was nothing half so simple as an event she could experience and draw a line under. Something that she could have once, then get over.

But it was too late now. And when he began to move inside her, she couldn't regret it. Not one bit. Pleasure built in her core as he thrust deep, over and over again.

She could feel his control beginning to slip, and she wanted it to. She kissed his neck, his ear.

He shuddered.

On instinct, she wrapped her legs around his waist, so she could take him in even deeper.

"Yes," she whispered.

He lowered his head, burying it in her neck.

And he thrust one last time as her orgasm unraveled her entirely. He groaned out his own release, his whole body shaking.

And then she held him. As he held her.

She wanted to stay. But she didn't know what his policy was on that. He was so against relationships and . . . she did have the animals.

"I should go," she said.

"You don't have to."

"I do, though. Because in the morning I'm going to have to get up really early and take care of all the critters."

He regarded her, his gaze steady. "What if Hank and I went to your place for the night? He's got his crate. So that should keep him away from the animals that don't care for him much."

Oh right. Pascal and Maleficent didn't like Hank. As if she needed another barrier between herself and Remy.

"That's really sweet," she said.

He touched her face. "It's not sweet. We were just together, and I wouldn't feel right about us sleeping apart tonight."

"Is that what you do with Everywoman? Or is that just me?"

The answer to that question probably wouldn't make her very happy. In truth, she shouldn't have asked it. But she had. Because she didn't have the fortitude to not ask.

"No. I don't spend the night with other women. But you're

not other women, Lydia. You're you. And you mean a hell of a lot to me."

"You mean a lot to me too."

But she knew she meant it in a deeper way than he did. She wasn't going to dwell on that. She wasn't going to let it hurt. So she let him pack Hank's crate up. Let him load everything into his truck and follow her back to her house.

When they opened the door, all her animals were beside themselves. Hank was on a leash, and Pascal paused on the counter to give him deadly raccoon side eye.

"Pascal," she said. "You need to behave yourself. He's not going to hurt you."

Hank really had proven to be a perfect gentleman in every venue he'd visited so far. He had been lovely to Wesley, and totally fine at her parents' house. But here, his size was an issue. He was making her poor wary animals nervous.

But they were going to have to get over it. Because Remy was going to be spending the night at her house. And Remy and Hank were a package deal.

Just as she came with . . . well, all this.

Pascal was highly irritated, his body language completely indignant.

"Sorry," she said.

And then Maleficent burst down the hallway, barking and barking, her Chihuahua rage knowing no bounds. Chewy loped behind her, entirely unbothered, as he always was. Lydia bent down and scooped Maleficent up. "Now," she said. "You're fine. Hank is nice."

From her high-up perch, Maleficent was entirely too confident. And when Lydia tried to lower her to greet Hank, she growled at him.

Hank, for his part, didn't react at all.

It wouldn't be fair to him to turn Maleficent loose on him.

Chewy and Hank sniffed each other, and Chewy went to lie on his bed after about thirty seconds of sniff introduction.

"I'm going to put her in her crate. I'll give her a Kong with some peanut butter in it, and maybe she won't feel so maligned."

"I guess I don't know the story of how all your different animals came to you."

"A lot of them were supposed to be temporary," she said. "But I couldn't let them go. I am the biggest cause of foster fails at the whole shelter. But I usually don't end up with dogs or cats because I'm smart enough not to take them in—I know I'll adopt them all. Maleficent and Chewy are the only two dogs I have. Maleficent got torn up by a couple of pit bulls that lived in her household. She still hasn't gotten over it."

"Who would?"

"She holds a grudge. And then there's Chewy. But he's the world's most docile yellow Lab."

"Yellow Labs are big," he said, gesturing to Chewy.

"Yes. It took her a while to warm up to him too."

"So she could warm up to Hank."

"Possibly. Pascal . . . The problem with wild animals is that they're so unpredictable. But I got him when he was so little, he still had his eyes closed. There have been some attempts made at rehabilitation, but he just doesn't see the point. He likes to be inside. He never really learned how to be a raccoon. At best, he's sort of a weird dog. But with hands."

"Yeah. I'm aware of the hands. I find them menacing."

"They really aren't. He's very sweet. He loves the dogs, but I think because they are an established pack, he's quite protective of the order of things. He's a bit of an old man. In the wild raccoons barely ever live this long. In captivity, though, they can get close to twenty years old. Like a pampered house cat."

"That's a very long time to have a raccoon."

"Well, I've had a whole decade with him, and another one won't be enough."

"It seems like a lot of work."

"It is. But . . . I often think that I was such a strange child, if I hadn't had a soft place, a soft nest to be in for most of my life, I would've been very unhappy. My parents were that soft place. It feels right to be a soft place for other creatures. The ones people don't want. The blind ferrets and the one-eyed chickens. The voles that need a place to recover, even just for a while. I know it doesn't make sense to most people but . . ."

"It's actually beautiful," he said, the earnestness in his eyes surprising her. "Because you're right. I know what it's like not to have a soft place. To be the kind of kid that nobody wants. I'm way too familiar with it. Sometimes a soft place is miraculous in ways that I can't even explain. It can change your whole outlook on life. On everything. If it hadn't been for your parents . . ."

"I'm glad they were there for you. But I hope you understand that when you really care about somebody, it's not a burden. I hate to compare you to a homeless raccoon, but Pascal's not a burden. All my time with him has been a gift to me. It's a funny thing. By making space for people and animals that need help, you're actually opening yourself up to the miraculous. My family is better for having had you in it."

He looked stunned by what she'd said.

"It's true," she said.

"Well, I appreciate that."

"I care about you," she said. Because she felt it needed to be said. "Not as a project or anything like that. And I didn't sleep with you just because I'm a sad late-twenties virgin. I actually wanted to."

He moved toward her, gripped her arm and pulled her toward him. "I slept with you because I wanted you. Not because

I owed you a favor, not just because you wanted to lose your virginity. Not even because the idea of some other guy doing it made me see red."

"Did it, though?"

"Hell yeah."

"Well, I'm kind of pleased about that."

"Don't be. Don't encourage me." He sighed heavily. "Pascal can't go back out to the wild."

"No. He's too . . . different. He's too used to being around people. He doesn't have the ability to survive on his own."

"Because sometimes, if you're small enough when the bad things happen, you can never really become what you were meant to be. You sort of think you're a dog, or whatever."

She felt a sliver of ice slip into her heart. "Yeah. I guess that's true."

"I might be like Pascal."

"I don't think so."

"I just want you to be aware of that. Because it has nothing to do with you. Just like Pascal's limitations have nothing to do with you. He's better off for having you. So am I. But . . ."

"How about this. You stop trying to anticipate what you need to say to me. You just let this happen."

He let out a long, slow breath, and she could see that it pained him. "Yeah. I guess I can do that."

"Good."

They made sure that all the animals were where they needed to be, separated from one another, and fed. Then she took Remington Lane into her bed. Into her arms.

But she couldn't tell him that she had also taken him into her heart.

Because he simply wasn't ready to hear it.

She had to hope that this was just the first step, and someday he would be.

Because if he was going to go ahead and use metaphors about animals, so was she.

She had never met a wounded animal that she didn't believe deep down she could fix.

She would fix him too.

Or she would break her own heart trying.

# Chapter 9

He and Lydia had been sleeping at each other's houses, back and forth, for four days now. He had, he could admit, avoided a couple of calls from Matthew because talking to his friend made him feel uncomfortable. As if Matthew would be able to see or hear the truth of the situation if they were to get on a voice or video call.

And there was no point having the discussion. He felt like a fool. Because sweet Lydia had given herself to him, and he found that every day he felt more like a feral dog she had taken in and fed. He didn't want to leave. But he also couldn't offer her anything. He just didn't know how.

But he was spending so much time with her these days that it was difficult to imagine what his life would look like when this ended.

He didn't want it to end. That was the honest truth. Little as he liked to admit it.

The day the horses arrived, Lydia was there with her hair in braids, a cowboy hat planted firmly on her head. She was wearing her usual jeans and a T-shirt and grinning from ear to ear.

He had never seen her quite so excited. And he had done a pretty good job of exciting her during their nights together, if he said so himself.

The condition of the horses that were led out of the trailers shocked him.

Even though they had been given good care these last few weeks, they still looked rough beyond telling.

He remembered that a couple of the horses that had been taken from his father's ranch couldn't even be saved. That said a lot about the condition they must've been in.

It was amazing how easy it was to see his father's cruelty when he was looking at animals.

And yet he had never really extended the same level of compassion to himself.

He had always felt as if in some regard maybe he hadn't been a very good son. Hadn't inspired his father to want to treat him well.

But these animals hadn't asked to belong to Hunter Lane. They simply had.

Just as he had.

Same as Pascal hadn't asked to be orphaned as a tiny raccoon, hadn't asked to be turned into a domestic creature who couldn't survive on his own.

He felt a surge of compassion rise up inside for his old self. The boy he'd been.

But the truth was, it didn't make him any more able to cope with the situation.

That was the saddest bit.

Feeling compassion, knowing something was wrong, didn't fix things. It didn't mean that everything could be put to rights as if it had never been wronged.

He was far too familiar with that truth.

But he had the horses now, and he would focus on them.

He got information about the special care and treatment

they would need for a while as they continued to build up their strength, shook hands with the people from the rescue, and then he stood there, contemplating yet more evidence of his father's general evil.

"You're a good man," Lydia said, patting his shoulder.

"I don't know if that's true. But I definitely feel that what happened to these creatures was unjust."

Hank had perked up when the horses had arrived. Now he ran out into the field. The horses seemed to know him. Hank ran around them in circles, looking younger than he ever had in the time that Remy had had him.

"Look at that," he said. "They're friends."

"I guess they were a soft place for each other. Even when the whole rest of life wasn't soft."

"I guess so."

He cleared his throat. He wished . . . he wished for something. So fiercely, deep down, that he could barely breathe.

His whole life had changed in the past couple of weeks. Since Lydia had shown up with Hank. His house felt fuller. His life felt fuller.

He felt . . . he wanted to feel hopeful. But it was just so damned difficult.

"What are you thinking about?"

"That I can't wait to go to bed tonight," he said, looking at her, his chest expanding.

She blushed. Then stretched up on her toes and kissed him. He wrapped his arms around her waist and kissed her back. "This has been good," he said.

It had been. He had never really had a relationship with a woman like this before. Never gotten to where he knew so much about her. Both naked and clothed. Had never shared space like this.

"I love you," she said, her eyes never leaving his.

He felt as if she had punched him in the gut. "What?"

"I love you, Remy. But I thought that was pretty obvious."

"No, it . . . It's not."

How the hell would he know what love looked like? No woman had ever looked at him and said that. No one had ever . . . No.

"I'm sorry. I thought that I could keep my feelings to myself. I thought that . . . I thought that I could just let this go on as it was. I know that's what you want. And actually . . . I don't want you to say anything. I don't want you to turn me away."

He didn't know what to say. Because of course he had been about to throw up all kinds of reasons why she couldn't love him. Why they couldn't be together. Of course he had been.

"I don't want you to tell me that I don't love you. Because I do. I have since long before you moved into my parents' house."

"You like a stray."

"I do," she said. "But I also know that just because a creature is a stray, it doesn't make them any less valuable. If my having all this love to give to creatures who need it makes you believe my love for you is less real . . . I feel sorry for you. Because look at men like your father. Who take animals in and then treat them terribly. He was bad to people, he was bad to animals. Just because I like strays, that doesn't make my love for you mean less."

"Lydia . . ."

"I told you. I don't want to hear it. I don't want to hear why you can't be with me. What I want is for you to sit with this. I want you to think on it. Because I deserve that much consideration. At least that's what I think. I love you. Like in love with you. I always have. When you moved into my parents' house, it was the single most glorious and hideous thing ever. Because I could be with my crush all the time, but also, you could see me in my pajamas. But now, you see me naked. In my pajamas. Looking a mess, looking good. We were already halfway there. That's why there hasn't been anyone for me. It's always been you. I have never been able to imagine myself with somebody else."

"I'm sorry," he said. And he meant it. Because it was a damn shame that this sweet, wonderful woman had never been able to imagine herself with another man because she had imprinted on him like a baby chicken way back when. She deserved more. More than him. A man who was scared to death of relationships of any kind. Hell.

"Don't," she said. "I don't want your regretful apologies. I don't want your sad-eyed rejection. What I want is for you to sit with yourself and tell me the real reason you don't think we can be together."

"Your family . . ."

"Loves you."

"Your brother is my best friend."

"Yes. And he loves you. He knows what a good guy you are. He never stops talking about it. You don't seem to understand that you gave something to us too. Do you have any idea how afraid Matthew was that his friends would reject him? Big tough guys that you all were. And some of them did."

"Those guys didn't matter. What kind of person gives a shit about who their friend loves?"

"A lot of people. But you don't. To the point you don't even understand why somebody would. You don't even understand that what you gave to him was real friendship. That it mattered. You're so stuck on the idea that you're a charity case, and that we didn't get anything from you. But it isn't true. We love you. All of us do. And you have been a gift to us. So sit with that. Don't worry about what my family will think, other than the fact that they really, really care about you. And then . . . get over yourself."

Then Lydia Clay turned and walked away, leaving him standing there with the animals that she had brought into his life, and an ache in his chest that hadn't existed before.

She had broken up with him, kind of. The ball was in his court.

But he had no idea what to do with it next.

# Chapter 10

Lydia called her brother before she was even halfway back home. "Just so you know, I slept with Remy. And he rejected me."

"Hold on," said Matthew. "What?"

"I . . . I slept with him. A while ago. And then just today I told him that I loved him, but you know he can't handle that."

Her brother made a noise that she had never heard him make before. It was almost a scream, halfway a growl, and also something sort of defeated and resigned. "That is just . . . I'm annoyed at both of you, to be honest."

"Why?"

"Because. He's a disaster, even though he's the greatest guy I know, and if he was going to get into a relationship with you, he really should have . . . because obviously you . . ."

"I obviously what?"

"I know you used to have a crush on him. I just didn't know that it persisted."

"Oh yeah. It persisted big-time."

"Well, I just wish you'd talked to me first."

"Why? So you could talk me out of it?"

"No. I would never . . . I would never try to tell you what to do. You're a grown woman. But I would've tried to . . . give you tips and tricks on how to handle him? Because he's the whole thing. And he's emotionally—"

"I know. I know he is. And actually, I think I handled it pretty well. It just hurts. And sucks. But I knew he wasn't going to be able to accept it. I told him I didn't care. I told him that I wanted him to sit with it and think about it. I didn't let him give me a whole spiel on how he can't love and whatever else."

"Well. You did pretty well."

"Thank you."

"He's an idiot."

"A hurt idiot," she said.

"You would be perfect for him. You have the patience for his idiocy. Only people in our family do."

She laughed. "I guess so. Don't say anything to him yet. I need him to sort his shit out on his own."

"Are you sure you don't want me to go over and punch him in the face for debauching you?"

"No. I asked him to."

"God damn, you're so *annoying*, Lydia."

"Yeah. I know."

There was silence for a moment.

"You're also very brave," he said. "Because it takes courage to go after what you want, even when you know it might hurt."

She nodded. "Yeah. I guess it does. So I'm a brave loser. At least there's that."

"No, Lydia. The losers are the ones who never try. Now he's going to have to prove that's not what he is."

Lydia marinated in that for the whole rest of the day.

# Chapter 11

Remy was miserable. And he had never felt quite so alone. Because he couldn't call Matthew, and obviously he couldn't call Lydia. Because the only other place he would go was the Clay house, but . . .

He found himself there anyway. His chest was sore, and he felt disappointed in himself. But it was just . . . She loved him. And it felt like such a big thing. It felt like something that could be explosive. Wonderful even. But terrifying. Hell. It felt so damned terrifying.

Because he'd never wanted somebody to be stuck with him the way he'd been stuck with his father. Because everything about domestic life, the very idea of it, terrified him. Unto his soul. He didn't mean to go see Nancy. He just ended up at that house. Ended up walking up the steps and knocking on the door. She opened it a moment later, wiping her hands on her apron. "Come in," she said.

"Can I get a hug?"

She pulled him in without any questions. And he just let her hold him for a second. He had so many things he wanted to ask her. He had so many questions, so many . . . so many things he didn't understand.

"Why don't you have a seat, and I'll make you a cup of tea."

"You might revise that offer when you find out why I'm here."

"I won't." She poured hot water out of her instant hot water tap, and stuck a teabag in it, sliding it across the table to him.

Express service, as if she knew this was an emotional emergency that needed immediate attention.

She sat down across from him and gave him the kind of maternal stare he had never gotten from anyone else. "What's going on, Remy?"

"For starters I . . . I'm cleaning up some of the mess my dad left behind, taking care of his animals. I'm just so angry at him. Because he was the one who should have taken care of them. Given them normal lives. And he couldn't do that one fucking thing. Sorry. Language, I know. But he couldn't. . . . And then I think . . ."

"He couldn't do it for you either," she said softly.

He shook his head. "No. And it would be easier if I hated him," he said, his chest aching as the revelation he had been avoiding rose to the surface.

"He's your father, Remy. It was never going to be that easy. You were born loving him. He probably beat a lot of it out of you. But you're a good person, with the capacity to care a whole lot. So of course, it's hard. Of course, your feelings are confused."

"It's more than confusing. It feels impossible. And I just . . . I know those animals didn't deserve the way he treated them. But sometimes it's hard for me to believe that I didn't deserve it."

"Of course it is. That's how every child in that situation feels. Because your parents are supposed to love you. But the problem was with them. Not with you. Think about it. There can't be a problem with you, and Hank, and those horses. Right?"

"No," he said.

"What's the other thing you wanted to talk to me about?"

He took a deep breath, his chest aching. "Lydia said she's in love with me. But it feels like . . . like it's not fair to her. Because she doesn't deserve some broken stray who has to learn how to be a husband or father. . . ."

"You listen to me," she said, moving her hand across the table, her expression never wavering, and not anywhere near as shocked as he had expected it to be. "Lydia has always known her own mind. I learned that I couldn't argue with her about the things she's passionate about the day she brought home a nest of baby squirrels and just about scared twenty years off my life with them. She is going to love the way she's going to love. And as fiercely as she's led to. You were denied a lot of love, and it seems to me that if you are lucky enough to have Lydia's, you should grab hold of it with both hands."

"But . . . don't you think I should maybe stay away from her? Don't you think I'm not really good enough for her?"

"I brought you into this house when you were a sixteen-year-old boy. And I had a young daughter who looked at you as if the sun, the moon and the stars were created by your very hand. I've always put a lot of trust in you."

He had never thought about it that way. Mostly because he hadn't realized that Lydia . . .

But even if she hadn't had a crush on him, he supposed it said a lot that her parents had been willing to let him move in with a teenage daughter in the house.

"You have proven to be a wonderful, honorable man. I couldn't ask for a better man for my daughter. If you love her."

He did love her. That was such an easy thing for him to identify. He did. How could anyone not love Lydia?

"But I don't know how to do all this."

"Well, you can provide for her financially," she pointed out.

"Yeah. But . . . I didn't grow up seeing a marriage function any kind of way. Not till I moved in here."

He half expected her to say that he should simply copy the Clays. But she didn't. "You imagine all the things you would've loved. The kind of love you would've wanted filling your house. And then you fill your house with it. Because it's your choice. Because your father is dead. He doesn't have power over you anymore. He doesn't get to decide what you deserve to have. That's the bottom line. You get to decide. If you love Lydia as much as she loves you, then live with her. Give her credit for being a strong, grown woman who can tell you what she wants. It doesn't have to be perfect."

"But I worry that if it's not, our relationship will only deteriorate. Because of my parents . . ."

"You're not your parents. Look at the life you've built. You're not your parents."

Lydia had already said that to him once. And so he was really left with only one reason why he couldn't be with her. Probably the truest thing.

"I'm just scared. Scared to want too much. And lose too much."

"I'll bet that Lydia would tell you the same thing that I'm about to. Because she has loved a whole host of animals, some of whom really were lost causes, though she'll never admit that. And I've given a lot of love in my life. To my own children, to my husband. To a teenage boy whose parents wasted themselves, wasted their lives by not loving. And I'll tell you, I have never been sorry for risking my heart. Not even one time."

Love filled him now. Certainty. A sense of stability. He had never really felt as if he belonged, but his loneliness had nothing to do with the Clays. It was him. Being too afraid to risk his heart.

But he could see what she was saying. He was keeping himself back. Allowing himself only as much happiness as his father had decided he ought to have.

He had gone to college. He had made his fortune.

Why shouldn't he have it all? Why shouldn't he have love?

"Thank you," he said. He stood up. "I have to go to Lydia. I . . . I love you."

Nancy went over to him and pulled him into a hug. "I love you too. It's been good to have you as a surrogate son. But I think I'd like to have you as a son-in-law even better."

Yes. That was what he wanted.

He had spent the better part of his life not caring what anyone thought.

But he cared desperately about this.

He was finally going to see it through.

Lydia heard a knock at her door, and she wondered if it was Matthew, come to commiserate.

It was very him to do that.

She got up off the couch, and all her animals descended upon the front door. "Stop, stop," she said over the barking and other noises of malcontent filling the air.

She jerked the door open, but it wasn't her brother on the other side. It was Remy.

"Oh."

"I thought it over. A lot. And most importantly, I talked to your mom. Because she's really the closest thing to a mother that I have. And I needed some guidance. I guess that's where I differ from a raccoon. I know that if I don't know how to do something, I can ask. Because I did have that soft place, Lydia. But I've been trying to exist outside it."

"You didn't have it easy."

"No. I didn't. But I had it better than most. Because I had your family. And I have you. Lydia, I love you. There's never been a question of that, actually. The way I love you has changed. It shifted. What I want from our relationship has changed. But my love . . . That's certain. And now I know I want to take the chance. I want to be with you. I want to marry you."

She gasped, backing up just slightly from the doorway, and he came in. The dogs were jumping up on him, but he didn't seem to care. Even Pascal reached toward him, and he didn't react. Because he was pulling her into his arms.

"I was scared. I was scared to care too much, because I was afraid I didn't deserve it and that you would eventually figure that out. I've been waiting for that. This whole time. But that's a bad way to live. I'm done with it. My parents don't get to decide how happy I'm going to be."

"Oh, Remy. I love you." She kissed him. Deep and long. She didn't feel so weird anymore. She felt right. Because the truth was, she had known. That he was the one. She had known before he had, and so no other man had seemed right.

It wasn't weird if it was love.

And this certainly was.

"I got some very good advice from your mom. She said that I need to listen to you. To love you. That we can change for the better. We don't have to get it perfect right now."

"I think we're going to be pretty perfect. The thing that I'm not sure about is . . . how we integrate all the animals. Mainly because of your aversion to raccoon hands."

"We could have five raccoons, and I wouldn't care. Because I love you. Not just the idea of you. And you come with all this."

There was nothing more wonderful that Remy could've ever said to her.

"Does that mean Pascal can be the ring bearer?"

"Absolutely not." He grinned and leaned in to kiss her. "I have to draw the line somewhere."

# Epilogue

It turned out, Remy wasn't as good at drawing lines with Lydia as he liked to believe. Because he ended up with Wesley as a ring bearer, all fine, and Pascal as a flower *critter*, which he was a lot less charmed by. Matthew was his best man. His total support of the union between Remy and his sister had filled Remy with a kind of joy that went beyond words.

It was mostly a Clay family affair. But they were his family now too.

And Lydia...

He stood at the altar, watching her walk toward him, wearing a white dress, just as she had been that night they first made love, with a bouquet of roses in her hands, and Hank walking right by her side.

Well, Lydia was more than just family.

She was a whole force of nature.

She had come in and changed his entire life, had expanded his idea of love from top to bottom.

And he was going to keep her, forever.

As she gazed up at him with eyes full of love, he felt a kind of peace that he had never imagined could be found by a man like him.

But that, he supposed, was the miracle of love.

It restored neglected horses and made abandoned cattle dogs into the most loyal of pets.

And it changed the hardest, most damaged of men into a father.

"Aren't you glad you took Hank in?" she asked just before he kissed the bride.

"I've never been gladder of anything in all my life. Except this." And then he kissed her, as his whole family, *her* whole family, cheered.

Remington Lane was entirely certain of what love was now. And that was a miracle he would never take for granted.

Please read on for excerpts from the authors' upcoming novels.

# THE GUEST COTTAGE

## Lori Foster

**In this uplifting series debut, forgiveness and unlikely friendship blossom in the haven of a quiet lakeside town when two very different women bond over one man's betrayals.**

Marlow Heddings is starting over. She's carried the outrage of her husband Dylan's affair with a younger woman—and the expectations of his family's powerful Chicago holdings company—long enough. Now, after another devastating twist of fate, she's unapologetically moving on.

Arriving in tiny Bramble, Kentucky, Marlow revels in her freedom, swapping her executive suits for sundresses . . . and scouting places to open her dream boutique. Best of all is her new residence, an adorable cottage with gorgeous lake views— and a breathtaking landlord, former Marine Cort Easton. Soon they're sharing dockside morning coffee and nighttime firefly gazing. Marlow's new life feels like a dream.

Then Pixie Nolan arrives on her doorstep. With a shocking secret.

To Marlow's astonishment, Dylan's "other woman" is a desperate girl of nineteen, destitute, exhausted, and disowned by her family. Defying her manipulative in-laws' demands, and surprising even herself, Marlow vows to lay down roots in Bramble and help Pixie get on her feet. Then they'll part ways. But empathy has a way of forging bonds. As Marlow grows close to the hardworking, devoted young woman, she becomes something of a big sister to Pixie.

Now, with each sunrise, Marlow awakens to the life she was truly meant to live, one filled with deepening connections, supportive friendship . . . and even a second chance at love.

# Chapter 1

The miserable May weather suited the occasion. At least the eulogy was over, and she no longer had to talk with Dylan's friends and distant family, all of whom expected her to weep for the loss of her dear, adoring husband.

Little did they know she'd lost him months ago when she'd found out about "the other woman." For Marlow Heddings, everything had ended that day, the love, the commitment . . . the farce. Her plans for the future.

Her mother-in-law, usually an unstoppable force but now somewhat fragile, wouldn't hear of having Dylan's name tainted, not even with the truth.

Yet the truth was never far from Marlow's mind. He'd been a lying, unfaithful, deceitful bastard. He'd hurt her, then mocked her with a cruel lack of remorse.

The awful things he'd said, the hateful way he'd blamed her, continued to rage like a tornado in her mind.

As if to reflect her dour thoughts, the skies grumbled, dark clouds tumbling over each other. Soon there would be another deluge.

If it would end this farce, she'd gladly be soaked.

Despite her foul thoughts, all of them accurate, she maintained her composed expression. Let them think it was inner strength that kept her eyes dry, her emotions in check. In reality, it was numbness.

Soon she'd drive away from her loss, her oppressive memories, and the determination of her suddenly clinging mother-in-law.

"Such a beautiful memorial service," Sandra Heddings declared between her not-so-quiet sobs. "Everyone is properly honoring him."

*Properly* honoring him? In a bid to keep her thoughts to herself, Marlow flattened her mouth. She wasn't heartless enough to add to Sandra's pain. Whatever failings her mother-in-law might have, loving her son wasn't one of them. She'd cherished Dylan, making him her entire world.

Unfortunately, during the month that Dylan had been gone, it seemed Sandra had turned her sights on Marlow in some bizarre attempt to cherish his legacy.

"Come on," Marlow whispered gently, her arm around the other woman. "Let's get out of this rain."

"I don't want to let him go." Turning into Marlow, Sandra squeezed her arms tight around her as wracking cries broke loose.

Desperately, Marlow glanced around for help, but many had already moved on. Aston, Dylan's father, stood over the grave site, his head bowed and his proud shoulders slumped in pain. The few relatives still braving the weather were gathered around him, leaving Marlow to tend to Sandra.

Her wide black umbrella wasn't sufficient to shelter them from the endless drizzling rain. God, she wanted this day over with. She wanted, needed, to wrap up her duty, her social obligations, so she could escape it all.

Sandra had wanted to delay the service until the weather

cleared, but Marlow knew if she'd put it off at all, she'd have broken down.

Because she was taller and sturdier than Sandra, Marlow was able to steer her back along the path. "That's it. One step at a time. You know how much Dylan loved you. He'd want you inside, warm and dry."

"Yes, he would. He was such a good son. So devoted to our family." Sandra's eyes slanted her way. "To the business."

Not always true. In many ways, Dylan had resented his mother. In other ways, he'd repeatedly disrespected her. His contribution to the business had been as a mere figurehead. He'd done very little actual work, even less after Marlow had caught him cheating.

With him and Marlow at odds, he'd repeatedly missed work, using the excuse that he wanted to avoid his wife's "volatile and hostile moods," even though she was always professional at work. Marlow had solved that for him by resigning her position and walking away.

She'd needed time alone to grieve the loss of her marriage and her future, and to start planning her next steps. The litigated divorce proceedings she'd begun almost a year ago had enraged all the Heddingses—Dylan, his mother, and his father. None of them had expected her to fight, which only proved how little they'd really known her.

She'd given a lot to her marriage, and she'd helped to build the assets she and her husband had accumulated. Taking what she'd earned was fair; she didn't want or need anything of Dylan's. Yet he'd disagreed, and the battle had begun.

Just as it seemed they might get the divorce finalized, Dylan had died.

Now, none of that family antagonism seemed to matter anymore. Not to a grieving mother. Sandra had adopted a "let bygones be bygones" attitude.

As Marlow patiently urged her mother-in-law along, her

gaze repeatedly swept the area. She half expected "the other woman" to show up. Wouldn't that be the perfect theatrical kick? A lone mysterious woman, dressed all in black, watching from afar?

But no, it was only Dylan's family and friends, all of them heartbroken that Saint Dylan was no longer with them.

Jaw locking, she lifted her chin a little higher and finally got her mother-in-law into the building. "Aston will bring around the car."

"This has destroyed him."

Yes, Dylan and his father had been close. Toasting each other at parties, golfing together. Dylan was supposed to inherit the family dynasty.

For the longest time Marlow had wanted children, but Dylan had refused, insisting that he wasn't yet ready. Now, she was grateful she didn't have a child that would tie her to these people. A decade of marriage had brought about familiar, if not openly affectionate, feelings, but she'd already decided that it was past time she cared for herself.

A while later, on the drive from the grave site, Marlow worked up her courage to set the wheels in motion. "I'll see you both home, but I'm not coming in."

Sandra had been weeping into her hands, but now her head jerked up and her tears miraculously dried. "What are you talking about? You're Dylan's wife. Of course, you're coming in."

In another few weeks, despite the way Dylan had fought her on everything, she would have been his ex-wife. Then he'd gotten himself killed in a car crash. Now she couldn't even make her grand exodus from the family. A divorce would have been the perfect exclamation point to her anger.

Instead, because she was a nice person, she was being forced to tiptoe away.

Nerves strung to the breaking point, Marlow shook her head. "It's better that I don't. I have my own plans to finalize now."

In an expression reminiscent of his son's, Aston scowled darkly. "What *plans*?"

He practically growled the word, but she'd expected this. Anything that didn't comfortably coincide with his itinerary was an annoyance. "I'm moving away." To a different house, in a different community, in another state.

A fresh start, away from grief and heartache.

Somehow during the ten years of her marriage, she'd completely lost herself. Gone was the happy, relaxed young woman she'd once been, replaced by a staid, conservative-dressing, matronly businesswoman whom, honestly, Marlow didn't even like.

If she couldn't even like herself, how had she expected Dylan to love her?

*Because he'd made her the person she'd become.* He'd made their major decisions as a couple. Where they'd live, how they'd live, and which social functions were advantageous. She'd *allowed* him to take the lead, to guide their marriage and their future. And in doing so, she'd morphed into someone different—an uptight, rigid woman who always followed the rules of etiquette and never caused a scene.

That nonsense was over.

"Don't be ridiculous," Aston said. "You'll reclaim your old job."

"No," she replied, softly but firmly. "I won't."

Sandra gave a shuddering sigh. "I understand why Dylan wanted you gone once you'd filed for divorce." Her look of censure showed through her sorrow. "I still don't understand how you could humiliate him like that."

Pride kept her voice even. "I will never settle for less than what I give."

Sandra waved her response away. "It was just a silly mistake."

"The woman meant nothing," Aston seconded with heat. "Less than nothing."

Their attitude no longer surprised Marlow. She'd had years of hearing his parents staunchly defend Dylan's every bad decision.

"She mattered to me. To our marriage."

Aston scoffed. "You were willing to throw away your life together because of one indiscretion? After Dylan gave you everything? After all *we've* given you?"

So many angry words danced through her thoughts. Things she wanted to say. Things she should have cleared up long ago. For her own sake, she held them back. "I wish you both nothing but the best."

They didn't return the sentiment.

Outrage overshadowing her heartache, Sandra's eyes narrowed. "You would actually abandon us now? When we need you most? When we're hurting so badly?"

Pointing out that she hurt, too, that she'd been hurting for months, wouldn't accomplish anything. "I'm sorry, but there's nothing more I can do for you."

Thank God, the limo driver had traversed the long curving drive to their sprawling home and stopped before the entry. Others had already arrived, and more cars pulled in behind them. Marlow scooted across the seat, not waiting for the door to be opened.

Sandra grabbed her arm, her small hand almost desperately tight. "When you filed for divorce, Dylan wanted you cut out of his inheritance."

"I know." Like a threat, he'd shouted his intentions at her. The sad part was that the need to avoid scandal and humiliation was what inspired him. Not love. He'd found it inconceivable that she, a plain businesswoman from an upper middle-class background, would dare to walk away from the incredible Dylan Heddings.

"We talked him out of it," Aston said with satisfaction. "Stay with the business and the money will still be yours."

What he meant was that she needed to go on playing the inconsolable wife. "It doesn't matter." She had her own accounts, in her name only. She neither needed nor wanted the Heddingses' money. There were many things she'd let slide over the years, but she'd always protected herself financially.

Maybe she'd retained some survival instincts after all.

The door opened and Marlow stepped out. It didn't matter that they were both hissing quiet demands at her. Or that she'd left her umbrella in the car and her upswept hair was immediately soaked by the downpour.

It didn't matter that others looked on in shock as she walked away, backbone straight and head held high.

Slowly, she inhaled. Fresh air. Freedom.

A new beginning.

It was time to return to her roots.

He answered on the second ring with a simple, "Hello."

"Mr. Easton?" Anticipation made her breathless as she loaded the last box of personal items into her Lexus SUV and closed the door. "It's Marlow Heddings."

"I recognized the number."

He had the deepest, darkest voice, no-nonsense and without inflection. She'd only called him . . . what? Five or six times over the past two months? Ugh, he probably thought she was stringing him along. *Please, please, please*, she thought. "The property I was interested in renting . . . Is it still available?"

"It is."

Breath left her in a whoosh. "I want it."

After the briefest pause, he said, "There've been two other interested parties, so I can't continue to hold it."

"No, I mean I want it *now*. Today." Sunrise turned the sky from dark purple to mauve. Sometime during the night, the storm had blown through, leaving everything wet and fresh, renewed. "I'll be on my way to you in the next few minutes."

"From Illinois?"

"Glencoe, yes. I think it's something like a six- or seven-hour drive so I'll have to stop a few times, but it's barely dawn now. I'll definitely be there before the end of the day." She wasn't certain of the exact travel time because the town barely showed on the map. With fewer than four hundred people living there, it would be an escape from everything familiar and just what she'd been looking for.

Mr. Easton greeted her news with silence. Whether it came of disbelief or surprise, she had no idea.

"Will that be a problem? When last we spoke, you said you had immediate occupancy."

"Same day is a little more immediate than I expected."

Marlow stopped, her heart stuttering to a near standstill. The steady drip-drip-drip of rainwater from the trees mingled with the sounds of birds rejoicing and the distant bark of a dog. It could be a new and exciting day—unless he altered her plans.

The very idea got her talking fast. "Did you do the credit report? The background check? Is there something else you need?" She hadn't slept after the funeral yesterday. No, she'd finished packing everything she might need to begin anew, and nothing else. She meant to leave behind her old life.

A prearranged estate manager would sell the rest of the belongings in the house, including Dylan's things. The house had already been listed for a respectable sum and the Realtor could show it without her.

She was free and clear. All she needed now was a place to stay.

Ready to convince him, Marlow opened the driver's-side door and got behind the wheel. "I'd like to pay you upfront for six months, but I'm happy to rent the place—" *Indefinitely.* Shaking her head, she amended her first, possibly overwhelming word choice, to the less ambitious, "For as long as it's available."

"Not just for the summer?"

God, she was botching this. "Is it only available in the summer?"

Another stretch of silence, and then, "It's available beyond that. You're sure you'll be here today?"

"Yes. Already in my car." She started the engine. "Pulling out of my driveway now."

"All right, Ms. Heddings. Everything in your application checked out. You have my number, so give me a call when you arrive, and I'll deliver the keys to you."

Gale-force relief rushed through her. "Thank you! Oh, this is wonderful. I can't wait to arrive." To start my new life.

Finally, things were looking up.

With a smile in his tone, he said, "Drive safely."

# RUSTLER MOUNTAIN

### Maisey Yates

The citizens of historic Rustler Mountain, Oregon, have a history as colorful as the Wild West itself. Most can trace their lineage back to the original settlers, and many remain divided into two camps: outlaws, or lawmen. But none more legendary than the Wilders and the Talbots . . .

Every year, thousands of people come through Rustler for the rodeo, historic home tours, old-fashioned candy making demonstrations, sharpshooter shows—and to see the site of the 1800s shootout in which notorious outlaw Austin Wilder was killed by Sheriff Lee Talbot. Now Millie Talbot, the sheriff's descendant, wants to bring back the town's Gold Rush Days. But she needs the current Austin Wilder's support to make her dream a reality . . .

The Wilders are rumored to be as true to their last name as their ancestors. Nonetheless, Austin is agreeable to helping Millie. But he wants something in return. Austin is working to clear his family name by writing the true history of his outlaw ancestors and Millie might just hold the key.

When Millie wrangles Austin into helping plan Gold Rush Days, he figures it's a chance to get to the truth of the past. . . . But when sparks start to fly between this bad boy and good girl, will either of them come out of it unscathed?

*Welcome to Rustler Mountain!*

*Founded in 1849, this California Gold Rush town sits only eight miles from the Oregon-California border and served as a home base for thousands of people who crossed the country to make a new fortune for themselves in the American West.*

*In spite of its gold rush history, Rustler Mountain is perhaps best known for being the town where one of the most dangerous outlaw gangs of the West was apprehended.*

*On this site in 1867, the notorious Austin Wilder—leader of the gang that was responsible for a string of stagecoach, bank and train robberies from 1845 to his death—was shot dead by Sheriff Lee Talbot on Main Street in front of the Rustler Mountain Saloon. His brothers and co-conspirators, Jesse and William, were arrested and tried for robbery and murder, then hanged on the courthouse lawn.*

*Butch Hancock, another member of the gang, escaped and was never caught.*

*The spirit of the Wild West, with its outlaws and heroes, lives on in Rustler Mountain to this day, where its well-preserved historic Main Street pays homage to the past.*

—plaque at the head of Main Street,
Rustler Mountain, Oregon

# Chapter 1

Millie Talbot had never been called brave.

Mousy, timid, plain, homely, missish. Yes. *Jilted*, perhaps. Brave, no.

But as Millie stood there staring at the ranch house that sat smack dab in the middle of the Wilder homestead, she thought she might be a little brave for coming there.

Austin Wilder was an outlaw, after all. Maybe not so much in the present moment, and maybe never in the way his five times great-grandfather had been, but he had certainly raised a significant amount of hell in his youth.

An apple that had fallen very close to the tree.

Rustler Mountain traded on its history, and as a result the lore and legends of the Wild West often felt closer to the present day than they might otherwise.

The town still felt divided the way it had been back then. Into the lawful and the lawless.

As a result, the Talbots didn't mix with the Wilders.

Ironic that now she needed him.

She'd been rehearsing the speech that would get him on her

side since yesterday, when she'd finally come to the conclusion that he and his family were her only options if she hoped to solve two of her current pressing problems.

She'd written the speech.

She'd discarded it.

*Help me, Austin Wilder, you're my only hope.*

All the girls in middle and high school had whispered about him. A bad-boy fantasy or something like that. He'd ridden his horse down Main Street, right into the high school once. Defiant and cocky as always.

She'd heard about it. She'd been in eighth grade, so she hadn't actually seen it.

It had been more common for him to ride his motorcycle into town with his brothers, Carson and Flynn, flanking him, their friend Dalton Wade bringing up the rear, the bikes so loud you couldn't hear anyone talking over the roar of the engines.

They'd had legendary brawls with the Hancocks, who were also descended from outlaws—but did not mix with the Wilders, for historic reasons—and had near showdowns in the streets with the good citizens of town.

Austin had been arrested for any number of petty crimes in his youth. Moonshining, vandalism and grand theft auto. Though he'd never been convicted due to a lack of evidence.

They were the Undesirable Element about town.

They had their own saloon, their own haunts and hangouts, just as the other faction in town did.

Of course that had made him and his brothers ripe for speculation with any teenage girl in town who was inclined toward men.

Almost.

Millie had never had bad-boy fantasies.

She was the ultimate good girl.

And if she didn't have the library in common with him, she never would have come here.

But that was the thing.

For all his crass-talking, hard-drinking, brawling ways, he had always been a patron of the Rustler Mountain Library.

In Rustler Mountain, there was the good and the bad, and never the twain shall meet.

Except at the library.

She clung to that now. Their common ground. The reason he might help her. The reason he would even know who she was.

She reminded herself of all that now as she tried to force herself to walk up the porch steps so she could knock on the door.

This meeting had seemed easier when it was theoretical.

Well, that was life.

Everything had seemed easy just two months ago. Now it was all different and terrible, and she was about to fling herself on the mercy of Austin Wilder.

Mercy she wasn't sure he possessed.

But he was a *reader*. That made her feel they had something in common. It made her feel she had a hope of reaching him.

When she was a girl, and her mother was the head librarian, she used to watch him from behind the reference desk. He always came in alone. He was about five years older than she, so he had always seemed tall and remote.

He still did, honestly.

He wore outlaw the way her father had worn his sheriff's badge.

Not surprising, because the town's history was emblazoned everywhere. Their bestselling souvenirs were bricks from the original red brick streets in town, which had been etched with the words: RUSTLER MOUNTAIN, LAST STOP FOR THE WILDER BROTHERS.

However, for all that the townspeople loved their history, the actual historical society was underfunded. The museum had closed a decade ago. It had once occupied the original court-house, which was now being used as a town hall, with all the wonderful artifacts in boxes in the basement.

Gold Rush Days, once a staple of town tourism, running all through the month of June, used to bring in schoolchildren and visitors from out of town to see living history, gold panning and a Wild West show, which included a reenactment of the last stand of Austin Wilder. The historical figure, not the man she was here to see.

She wanted them back. Those events had been the pride and joy of her father, and he'd wanted to see them restored.

Something Millie was working on.

But Millie needed votes. Votes she would have had if her now ex-fiancé hadn't cheated on her with Danielle LeFevre, the daughter of the former mayor, now town mayor, herself.

The way voting on town matters worked in Rustler Mountain was . . . quirky was maybe a nice way of saying it.

Town council members had votes, but so did members of Rustler Mountain's founding families.

When she and Michael were engaged, she'd had enough votes. Michael was a Hall. The five times great-grandson of Rustler Mountain's first banker. Michael was friends with the Langleys and the Hugheses, and they would generally vote with him. She could no longer count on those votes.

But the vote it hurt worst to lose was her father's.

He'd died two and a half months earlier. The loss was fresh enough that there were still days she found herself standing there washing dishes or pruning the roses in her front yard, or putting a book back on the shelf at the library, and she'd be jolted by the sudden realization that John Talbot was dead.

She'd lost her mother ten years earlier, so she was no stranger to loss.

But with her dad gone . . .

She was the last remaining Talbot in town.

And it seemed that without him, she didn't matter at all.

It certainly didn't help that right after his death, she'd found out Michael was cheating with Danielle, and her wedding had been called off and . . .

Well, here she was.

Danielle was also a member of a founding family and had run on a platform of building Rustler Mountain up, but her idea of the way to go about it was very, very different from what Millie thought needed to happen. She proposed that the part of the budget Millie wanted for the historical society should be "earmarked for town council travel."

Millie had four members of the town council on her side, as well as the Millses, the Bowlings and the Lins.

She and her opposition were dead even.

And that was where Austin came in.

She needed the Wilder vote.

She could only hope that she was right in thinking she might be able to get it.

She doubted that anyone in town would believe her if she told them that he was a regular at the library.

But he had been since he was a boy, and he remained one now.

They didn't speak when he came in. But he did come, once every two weeks, and he spent an hour or so perusing the shelves, coming back to the desk with a stack of books of just about every imaginable variety.

Around town, Austin had a reputation for being remote, cold and hard. For being, essentially, the reincarnation of his ancestor.

He'd changed, though, after his father's death, after his half sister had come to live with him and his brothers. The brawls had stopped.

But the town's memory was more than a century long, so his reputation remained.

Austin had already lived longer than his father, his grandfather and his great-grandfather. Who had basically all lived just long enough to procreate, and then gotten themselves killed doing something dangerous or illegal.

She had to hope there was more to Austin than that. She wanted his vote.

She also wanted some artifacts from his family for the museum. If she could go into that meeting with his vote and with offerings of new attractions and insights for the grand reopening of the museum, she would feel . . .

Well, she would feel like maybe she was a Talbot in more than just name.

Austin's family had a legacy of living fast and dying young. Hers was a legacy of staying strong and steady. Millie often didn't feel strong or steady.

She needed to be now.

"Have courage," she whispered to herself as she walked up the steps. She could have used his phone number. She had it in the library system.

But she felt that would be a violation of her sacred librarianship vows.

Not that she had actually taken *vows*, but she did take her job very seriously. The truth was, she knew which books everyone in town checked out. With knowledge came power and great responsibility. She had to be vigilant. She couldn't just go telling everybody that Ronald Miller had checked out a book on herbal remedies for erectile dysfunction.

She simply had to check the book out, keep her expression neutral and perhaps murmur a couple of things about the weather.

She did not ever say anything about the weather to Austin Wilder, however.

She took a breath, and gathered herself up, stomping up the porch steps, trying to use the vigorous nature of her steps to boost herself up.

Then she knocked. Firmly.

She was coming here to talk about the town. The past and the future.

She cared about both with all that she was.

A little ember began to burn in her chest.

She might be mousy a lot of the time, it was true. She couldn't deny it. But when she got started talking about subjects she felt passionate about, she found her fire.

She was passionate about *this*.

And maybe passionate about beating Michael.

Maybe.

She waited for a moment, listening for the sounds of footsteps after she knocked.

She heard nothing.

She knocked again.

"Can I help you?"

She whirled around, putting her hand on her chest as if it might catch her heart as it tried to slam its way past her breastbone. "Oh," she said.

There he was, standing in the dust behind her, cowboy hat planted firmly on his head, cowboy boots planted firmly on the ground.

He was wearing battered blue jeans, and a belt with an ornate buckle. His expression was unreadable, his square jaw set firm, his mouth a grim line. His dark brows were locked together, eyes glittering with emotion she couldn't name.

He was backlit by the sun filtering through the towering pines behind him, and he looked as dangerous as he was rumored to be, as the many generations of his family were always purported to be.

"Austin?"

He looked her up and down, his gaze bracing.

"You're the librarian," he said.

At least he recognized her. She sometimes had the sense that she was nothing more than floral wallpaper to the men of this town. Even to her own fiancé.

Who hadn't even noticed her when she'd walked in on him with . . .

She didn't need to reflect on that right now.

"Yes. I am. I . . ." She cleared her throat and tilted her chin upward. "That's not what I'm here about."

He was so tall. So broad. And somehow it felt very different to be staring him down here, without the reference desk between them.

That, she realized, was her territory, and he, the outlaw, was a trespasser in it.

Here?

She was the one who didn't belong.

She swallowed hard.

"I was going to say, I know I don't have anything overdue."

"We don't make door-to-door attempts at repossessing books, Mr. Wilder."

He snorted. "No one in my family has ever rated the respect of being called *mister*. Just call me Austin."

It wasn't an overture of friendliness, but a flat statement of fact. She didn't know quite what to make of it. "Okay."

"What brings you up to Wilder Mountain if you aren't here to repossess a copy of *The Life-Changing Magic of Tidying Up*?"

"You . . . you turned that in two weeks ago." She clasped her hands up at the center of her chest. Someone in high school had once said she made "mouse hands" when she was nervous, and every time she caught herself doing it, it infuriated her.

She lowered them quickly.

"So I did." He stood there, staring, making her feel tiny even though he was standing down on the ground gazing up at her on the porch.

"You have *The Elements of Style* and a Jack Reacher book right now," she said.

"I actually do know which books I have out right now."

"Right. Well. I came up here because I wanted to talk to you. About . . . I'd like to ask you about a couple of things. The first is that I'd like to talk to you about any artifacts—journals, letters or family heirlooms—you might be willing to donate to a new endeavor I'm working on."

He crossed his arms across his broad chest, and she couldn't help but notice how muscular his forearms were. And his chest under the tight white T-shirt he wore. Which was a silly observation, really. He was a cowboy. A working man. Of course he had muscles.

The heaviest thing she lifted was a weighty reference book.

He frowned. "Why?"

"I want . . . I want to reopen the museum. I have so many documents in the library. Historical journals and newspapers. All the artifacts that used to be on display at the courthouse are just gathering dust and . . . maybe I could put them on display at the library or in a different building in town—I'm still working on that part—but I want to have this information available again."

"Then what do you need me for?"

"I'm a Talbot. The stories I have about my family, whether lore, legend or fact . . . They are innumerable. But when it comes to the Wilders, there's nothing but speculation."

"And you want what?" He huffed. "Our side of the story?"

"Well . . . yes."

"Make no mistake, Miss Talbot, what you really want is a boogeyman. You like your heroes and your villains, and you don't like it complicated."

"That isn't true," she said. "I want to portray the real history of the town."

"And so you're done with reenactments of my ancestors being shot in the streets?"

Her mouth dropped open, and then she shut it again. "I have no control over a private company's Wild West shows."

"I'm not asking about the Hancocks' Wild West Show.

Their historically inaccurate nonsense is their own concern. Their family never had scruples and I don't expect them to have any now. What I'm talking about is the Historical Society–sanctioned reenactment of the showdown that occurs under the guise of education."

"I . . ." She stumbled over her words. "That's part of the other piece of the conversation."

"We've never spoken more than four words to each other, and you have two favors you want to ask? Damn, darlin', that is bold."

She knew that wasn't supposed to be a compliment, but she took it as one all the same. "I need to be a little bold with this one, so I thought I'd take a shot."

"Oh, careful. I find that triggering. Considering a Talbot did in fact shoot my ancestor."

"Sorry," she said quickly.

For the first time she wondered what it was like to have your family history centered on being the one who was shot dead.

She was related to the one who'd done the shooting.

"I'm kidding," he said. Then he sighed heavily. "Come on inside."

He walked up the porch steps, and then past her. She could smell hay, sweat and something indefinable on the wind as he moved by her. It didn't smell bad.

On the contrary, he smelled like the land. Like hard work and sunshine. Like dirt and trees.

It made her heart trip over itself, but she quickly gathered her wits. Austin Wilder was the kind of man who turned female heads wherever he went. It was impossible to ignore him. But one thing Millie had going for her—she was focused.

And she would remain focused now.

He held the door open and led her inside the house. She wasn't sure what she had been expecting, but she found herself fascinated by this place. It was clean. A large open space, a living room, kitchen and dining area all combined into one. There was a large bookshelf next to an overstuffed chair. Everything was old, well-worn, but scrupulously kept.

She didn't think there was a speck of dust to be found in the whole place, and it was just . . . Not at all what she had expected from a rancher who was descended from one of the Wild West's most notorious outlaws.

For a man with a tarnished reputation, he kept a very clean house.

"Have a seat," he said, gesturing to a spot at the square oak dining table.

There was no décor in the place, nothing that spoke of whimsy. A wooden floor, the walls covered in wood paneling, the ceiling also wood, with large log beams.

There were blinds, not curtains, over the window. And there wasn't so much as a throw pillow on the couch. No vases with flowers, or anything like that.

It was nearly military, all that cleanliness combined with the simplicity.

"So what makes you think this is something the town wants? Something you can be successful with."

"I think you misunderstand me. This isn't a moneymaking venture. We have a building. The Talbot family. And I want to use it for this. The library is already in possession of a great many documents that I can use. But what I really want is to make the exhibit as interactive as possible. And I want people to get a deeper look at the reality of this place."

"All right. And to do that you want . . . to go through all my family's old shit?"

"Yes. And you know, if you . . . have any heirlooms you might possibly be interested in donating."

"We have a collection of things in the attic."

"They're labeled and sorted, aren't they?" she asked.

Because she could see it. He took good care of what he had.

He was an enigma, Austin Wilder. A man who read books, had a meticulously clean home, everything in its place, and yet possessed an outlaw reputation.

"They are," he confirmed. "How did you guess?"

"You seem like the type."

He chuckled. "Most people would say that I don't."

"Most people haven't watched you check books out for the last twenty years."

He laughed dryly. "Fair enough. So when you put forward your plan for the new museum, you're confident that the town council is going to approve it? We both know they have a chokehold on what happens on Main Street."

"Yes," she said, "they do and . . . that's where I need . . . my second favor."

"Your second favor relates to the town council," he said, the words deadpan.

"Yes."

"Just how do you think I can help you with a whole panel of people who think I'm as bad as every other Wilder who came before me?"

She cleared her throat. "It doesn't matter what they think. You have the vote. The founding family vote."

He rubbed his chin, and the sound of his whiskers scraping against his palm sent an electric response all down her spine. "I see. So you don't just want to take my family heirlooms and journals to make a museum. You want me to physically come and exercise a vote I've chosen never to exercise even once."

Well, when he put it like that.

"I was hoping you might," she said.

"All for what? For your family's continued glory?"

"I told you," she said, sputtering now. "I . . . I don't want that. I want to present history in a real way and—"

"And continue with your sensationalized Wild West shows."

"They aren't *mine*," she said.

"You're a Talbot."

As if that was that.

"And you're a Wilder but—"

"I think you can see yourself out," he said.

She was so shocked that she almost couldn't comprehend what he'd just said. "What?"

"You heard me. You can see yourself out."

"I . . . I . . ."

"Is no not enough? Then how about *hell* no."

And with that, he stood up and gestured toward the door. And Millie Talbot found herself right back out on the front porch with no artifacts, no ally and no hope.

Visit our website at
**KensingtonBooks.com**
to sign up for our newsletters, read
more from your favorite authors, see
books by series, view reading group
guides, and more!

Become a Part of Our
**Between the Chapters Book Club**
Community and Join the Conversation

Submit your book review for a chance to win exclusive
Between the Chapters swag you can't get anywhere else!
https://www.kensingtonbooks.com/pages/review/